KILLER ON THE WARBUCKET

KILLER ON THE WARBUCKET

Ray Hogan

Chivers Press • G.K. Hall & Co.
Bath, Avon, England Thorndike, Maine USA

This Large Print edition is published by Chivers Press, England, and by G.K. Hall & Co., USA.

Published in 1996 in the U.K. by arrangement with the author.

Published in 1995 in the U.S. by arrangement with Donald MacCampbell, Inc.

U.K. Hardcover ISBN 0–7451–2882–3 (Chivers Large Print)
U.S. Softcover   ISBN 0–7838–1282–5 (Nightingale Collection
                                                              Edition)

The text of this Large Print edition is unabridged.
Other aspects of the book may vary from the original edition.

Set in 16 pt. New Times Roman.

Printed in Great Britain on acid-free paper.

British Library Cataloguing in Publication Data available

Library of Congress Cataloging-in-Publication Data

Hogan, Ray, 1908–
    Killer on the warbucket / Ray Hogan.
        p.   cm.
    ISBN 0–7838–1282–5 (lg print : lsc).
    1. Large type books.   I. Title.
[PS3558.O3473K54   1995]
813′.54—dc20   95–11096

CHAPTER ONE

What gets into a man, sets him to drifting?

That question trickled through Ben Kyle's mind as he topped the last rise and halted for his first look, after seven years, at his homeland.

He was on the fringe of Red Rye Flat, a broad, grassy, grove-spotted plain that stretched for miles to all directions. Far to the west, and curving inward on the north, the towering Sage Mountains formed a ragged, natural termination; to the east the Warbucket River, wide and often deep, laid its sparkling boundary—incidentally affording the town of Oak Springs its reason for existence where the bridge spanned the continuous flow.

Within that rectangle lay the ranches—Sanders' directly ahead, his father's place next and nearer to the mountains; and beyond were Melrose's and Reagen's and Schultz's, and several he could not recall. Midway, to his right and not far from the Warbucket, sprawled the only scar in an otherwise perfect land: an irregular shaped area of dry washes and ravines scooped from the range and filled with head-high brush and other wild growth. The Brake some called it, others termed it the Badlands, but for all it was trouble.

A man would have to be a fool to turn his

1

back on country like this, Ben decided, and reckoned wryly that he was such a fool. But he hadn't thought so that day when, with Henry Kyle's blessing, he had saddled his horse and ridden off to see what lay beyond the hills. He'd just turned eighteen and the drive within him wouldn't be denied.

'Something you'll have to get out of your guts,' his father had said. 'I know . . . And when it's done, come back. Me and the ranch'll be waiting.'

And so for seven years Ben Kyle had looked and searched and discovered that one side of a hill looked much like the other, that towns varied only in size, that in people there was little basic difference.

But Ben Kyle had learned much. After two years with the Texas Cavalry fighting for a hopeless cause in a senseless war, a stint at gambling, innumerable jobs riding the range; a time as a deputy sheriff in a trail town—it all added up to nothing more than experience. And then one day he'd had enough.

He was ramrodding for Gale Haig in the Rock Springs country of Wyoming. At the end of the month he had simply walked in, told Haig he was quitting, that he was going home.

Haig, a wise old man who said little but noticed much, merely nodded. 'Figured it was coming to this,' he said, and paid off. 'Good luck.'

Then had followed the long ride across

2

Colorado, down into New Mexico Territory, and finally he was on the edge of Red Rye Flat. It all looked good, felt good, and Ben Kyle had no regrets.

He was looking forward to seeing his father again. Henry had been crowding sixty—he'd be well on the way to seventy now—and he'd be equally pleased at the return of the prodigal and with the knowledge that his only son had gotten the trail dust out of his blood, was at last ready to settle down.

The Kyle ranch had never been much, mainly because Henry had entertained no dreams of empire. Good grass, plentiful water, winters made pleasant by the protecting hills to the north, were enough to satisfy him. He raised cattle enough for his own needs, doing most of the work himself—three hired hands were the most Ben could ever remember—and when he passed on he would be departing a gracious, easygoing life that many in the Warbucket country had found difficult to understand.

Perhaps there was much of Henry Kyle in his son; possibly he saw himself in Ben, recognized the errant forces that had plagued himself in his early years and therefore had a deep understanding of the boy's feelings. Such could account for his willingness to sanction Ben's desire to leave at an early age and lay no restraint upon him.

Ben had wished often he had kept in touch

with his father and several times had made up his mind to either ride by and spend a day or two, or at least write a letter. Somehow he had never gotten around to doing anything. Twice, when he had been in the general area, he had been trail bossing a drive and couldn't get away—and writing was always a laborious chore.

It didn't matter now.

He was home—back to stay. Ben raised himself on the saddle, easing his muscles while he stared out across the Flat. He was much too far to see the Kyle place, but on the far side, in a cup formed by sheltering buttes and slopes, was his father's holding. In another hour or two . . .

He settled back, swiped at the sweat on his forehead with the back of a hand. Reaching down, he adjusted the worn-handled Colt forty-five hanging on his hip to a more comfortable angle. It would be good to get home, sleep in a bed, have a roof overhead, eat regular meals, and know exactly where he stood and for what reason.

The adobe house Henry Kyle had built was always cool in summer, warm in winter, and there was never a time—

Ben's thoughts came to a halt as the dull thud of hooves brought him to attention. The sound came from a narrow, long running stand of cedars and rabbit-brush to his left. Instinct and habit threw him instantly into a state of caution; he reached down again, adjusted the weapon at his side.

Abruptly he smiled, shrugged; where did he imagine he was—back in a Texas range war? He was home. This was Red Rye Flat, in the Warbucket River country, not a place where a man had to keep a watchful eye on his backtrail and a hand always near his gun.

Easing his taut frame, he watched four riders break from the trees, spread into a line and advance slowly. One, a large, red-haired, ruddy-faced individual on a powerful black, was slightly in the lead. To his right was a younger and smaller duplication, undoubtedly his son.

On the opposite side was a thin-faced, dark man with a remote, detached manner and cool, deep-pocketed eyes. The fourth member of the party was young, like the son, but the servile manner that cloaked him tabbed him as a lackey.

All were strangers to Ben Kyle, but he guessed that was to be expected. Things would change in seven years. Silent, he watched them approach, fan out to form a half circle before him. When they drew to a halt, he nodded.

'Mornin'.'

The big man on the black rested both hands on the saddle horn, leaned forward. He gave Ben a hard, sweeping glance.

'Just what the hell you doing on my land, mister?' he demanded harshly.

CHAPTER TWO

Ben Kyle's features stiffened into cold lines. He studied the men gathered about him, gauging their possibilities, feeling the steady push of their hostility. The quiet one was where the danger would lie.

'Last I heard this was open range,' he said. 'Anyway, no man I know in this country faults another for just riding across his land.'

'You heard wrong,' the redhead snapped. 'Halverson range is closed to everybody except the Halversons.'

'And you're Halverson, I take it.'

The big man nodded curtly. He motioned at his younger likeness. 'So's he. My son—Bud.'

Halverson made no introduction of the two others; apparently in his reckonings, being only hired hands, they counted for naught.

'Now turn that horse around and head back the other way. You've gone far as you're going in this direction.'

Ben's cold gaze did not waver, and a dull anger was beginning to build within him. He was following the most direct route to his father's ranch, but he could swing wide and circle the Flat. Such would require no more than an extra hour's ride, but Halverson's manner was rubbing him wrong.

'Guess not,' he drawled. 'Like I said, this is

open range. People start listening to somebody like you, pretty soon a man won't be able to get out of his own yard.'

Halverson's face turned a darker red as anger rushed through him. 'Just who the hell you think you're talking to!'

'Seems your name's Halverson.'

The big redhead's color graduated to a livid purple. 'I'll—I'll—' he began in a trembling voice.

'Better take it easy, Park,' the quiet man broke in gently.

Halverson jerked back, made a quick motion with his hand. 'Keep out of this, Zuda!' he snapped, again in control of his temper. 'I'll handle this.'

Zuda shrugged, folded his arms across his chest. Bud Halverson frowned and the young rider next to him watched unsmilingly. The rancher fixed his eyes on Kyle.

'You aiming to defy me?'

'Not turning around, if that's what you mean,' Ben Kyle said, and roweling his sorrel lightly, started to move by Zuda.

'Stop him!' Halverson shouted, spurring in close.

Kyle's pistol came up fast—and then he felt the hard pressure of a gun barrel in his back. The young rider siding Bud Halverson had acted quick, rushed in from the rear. Ben lowered his weapon, slid it back into its holster.

'Good boy, Lonnie,' Park Halverson said

7

approvingly in the way a man might reward a terrier. 'Like to see you're on your toes.'

Lonnie grinned broadly. 'Yes, sir, Mr Halverson.'

The rancher bucked his head at Ben. 'Step down.'

Kyle hesitated a moment, then swung slowly from his horse, his glance never leaving the redhead.

'Get his gun, Dave.'

Zuda dismounted silently, lifted Ben's forty-five, thrust it under his belt and stepped away. Halverson turned to his son.

'All right, boy. Let's see you go to work the way I taught you. You're giving this saddlebum a lesson he ain't going to forget.'

'Sure, Pa,' Bud answered hastily and dropped to the ground. Glancing at Lonnie, he hung his hat on the saddle, wheeled to face Ben. Lonnie, also dismounting, moved in behind.

'Bud can do it alone,' Park Halverson said, lazily throwing one leg across the horn. 'Was me who taught him how to use his fists. Leave him be.'

Lonnie hesitantly fell back a step. Ben watched the faint grin fade from Bud's lips and an uneasiness come into his eyes.

'You sure you want this?' Ben asked, deliberate irony in his voice.

Bud said nothing, but the skin around his mouth tightened. Understanding moved Kyle.

8

The son was not like the father, a browbeating, hot-tempered bully, but he was thoroughly under the old man's thumb and trying to live up to expectations.

'Get at it, boy,' Park urged impatiently. 'Want everybody in this country to know the Halversons ain't to be trifled with.'

Obediently Bud lunged, swung wildly with his right fist. Kyle sidestepped easily, touched the other men with a veiled glance. He allowed the younger Halverson to recover, wheel, rush in again.

'Hit him—Goddammit!' Park shouted angrily as Ben parried the blow. 'What's the matter with you?'

A strange, frustrated expression crossed Bud's features. He spun, tried again to land a solid punch. Kyle, stepping in quick, blocked Bud's arm, drove his balled fist into the young man's belly.

Bud gasped, buckled forward. Instantly Ben seized him by the shoulder, spun him about and wrenched the ivory handled pistol from his holster. Then, shoving Bud at Lonnie, he smiled grimly at the men.

'Just don't make the wrong move,' he said quietly, 'and nobody'll get hurt.'

Park Halverson wrenched himself violently around on the saddle. 'Ain't no man pulls a gun on me—'

Kyle pressed off a quick shot. Halverson flinched as the bullet clipped the brim of his

9

hat.

'Always a first time,' Ben said coolly. 'Get off that horse.'

The rancher, flinging a desperate glance to Dave Zuda standing nearby, arms upraised, dropped to the ground. He stood motionless, huge, ham-like fists clenched at his sides, eyes burning with outraged fury.

'You—you ... By God, I'll—'

'You'll do what you're told!' Kyle snarled. 'Turn around—all of you!'

Halverson and the others complied slowly. Weapon ready, Ben moved up behind Dave Zuda, recovered his own pistol, relieved Zuda of his. Then disarming Park and Lonnie, he stepped back.

'Over there—by that stump,' he directed, pointing to a lightning-shattered cedar a few paces beyond the horses.

When the men had crossed to the designated point, Ben stepped to Halverson's black, dumped the weapons he had collected into one of the saddlebags.

'I'll run you down—make you pay for this!' the big rancher warned. 'Don't think you can get away!'

'Won't be hard to find,' Kyle said. Taking up the reins of the black, he collected the leathers of the remaining horses and holding them in his left hand climbed onto his sorrel.

Dave Zuda's jaw hardened. 'You leaving us afoot? Hell, we're ten miles from the ranch.'

10

Ben motioned with his pistol at a clump of trees some distance ahead on the Flat. 'Find your horses there,' he said and, tugging at the handful of reins, put the sorrel into motion.

*   *   *

Park Halverson, chest heaving in helpless anger, watched Ben Kyle ride off leading his small cavalcade of horses.

'Stop him—damn it!' he shouted. 'I ain't letting him get away with this!'

Zuda smiled bleakly. 'Stop him with what?'

Halverson seemed not to hear. He spun to Bud, standing just beyond Lonnie. 'This is your doing!' he yelled. 'Any damn fool'd a known better'n to tackle a man with his gun still on! Ain't you ever going to get any sense?'

Bud looked down, face pale. 'Just never thought, Pa.'

'Never thought! That's sure as hell the truth! You never think of nothing! Trying to teach you how to be a man is turning into a waste of time. And you,' he added, shifting his rage to Lonnie. 'Why wasn't you in there giving Bud a hand? What I'm paying you for, ain't it?'

Lonnie's mouth gaped. 'You told me—'

'Know what I told you—but when you saw Bud was needing help...'

Park Halverson's words died in a grumbling of exasperated oaths. He squinted across the sunlight-flooded plain at the slowly

11

diminishing figure of Ben Kyle and then turned to Zuda.

'And you—just what was holding you back? You're supposed to be so Goddammed fast with your iron!'

'Same thing that held Lonnie: you said to leave it up to Bud.'

'Expect my hired hands to pitch in when they see something that needs doing. Can't do it all myself.'

Zuda shrugged. 'You had the same chance as me. When he got his hands on Bud's gun, was too late.'

Halverson stared thoughtfully at the smaller man. 'I'm wondering if you're good as you claim you are. Any hired gun I ever heard of would have made some kind of play.'

'My job's to keep you alive, not get myself killed,' Zuda said mildly. 'Anyway, you'll get your chance again—if you want it.'

Halverson's lips parted to reply, checked. He looked more closely at Zuda. 'What's that mean?'

'He'll be around.'

'That drifter? You know him?'

'Didn't recognize him at first, then it come to me. Recollect seeing him a couple, three times when I was working for Hans Schultz.' Dave Zuda stared thoughtfully at the distant figure of Kyle leading the small group of horses. 'Appears the old man's cub's turned into a full growed catamount.'

'Old man!' Halverson roared impatiently. 'What old man? What the hell are you talking about?'

'Henry Kyle. That's his kid. Ben—I think they called him.'

Park Halverson frowned. 'Didn't know Henry had a son.' He glanced to Lonnie. 'You know him, too?'

The young rider wagged his head. 'Sure don't. Must've left here before I come.'

'Been gone six, maybe seven year,' Zuda said. 'Henry never talked much about him.'

The rancher's attention swiveled to the Flat. 'He was heading for the old man's place.'

'Reckon he was,' Zuda said. 'You ain't going to find him as easy to handle as you did Henry.'

Park Halverson smashed a thick fist into his open palm. 'They can all be handled ... one way or another,' he said. 'Come on, we might as well start walking. Them horses ain't going to get no closer.'

CHAPTER THREE

Ben Kyle glanced over his shoulder. Halverson and his party still stood by the blackened cedar where he had left them, were talking among themselves. He'd made no friends that time, he thought wryly, but it didn't disturb him

13

particularly. During his wandering he'd met plenty of the Halverson breed—big, powerful autocrats who fancied themselves King of the Mountain in their own little corner—and survived. He reckoned he'd survive Park Halverson, too.

He felt sorry for the son, however. Bud appeared to be a fairly decent sort, or he could be, at least, if left to his own devices. But he was having little to say about it. Park was doing his utmost to bend the boy to his will, mold him in his own likeness. And Bud, in turn, was striving to fit that mold.

But there was a vast difference in the two despite a similarity in looks. Bud would never acquire the savagery and ruthlessness Ben had seen flaming within the older Halverson; he was made of different stuff.

Ben reached the clump of trees, halted well within the shade. Dismounting, he anchored the horses at separate points where they could graze while they waited, and looked again to his backtrail. Halverson and the others had begun the trek across the Flat. Ben grinned, stepped back onto the saddle. It would be a hot walk for them. His smiled broadened as he visualized Park Halverson, roaring mad and cursing every step.

Wheeling the sorrel about, he cut through the grove, broke out again into open country, and continued north. Once off Red Rye he'd be near Kyle property, and he was growing

14

anxious for his first look at the land. From the general appearance of the Warbucket country, he guessed the spring had been a good one with several hard rains to soften the earth and fill the creeks and river.

If true, Kyle range should be in excellent condition. Ben hoped so. Plans for the future had been taking shape in his mind—plans that called for a system of confined grazing to add weight to the steers, and then sales to a buyer he'd become close friends with at the railhead in Dalhart.

He glanced to the sun. Shortly after noon. He'd be a bit late for the midday meal, but it wouldn't matter; Pa'd be glad to see him regardless of when he arrived. They had a lot of catching up to do once together again. And he had some making up to do, too, he thought, seven years' worth.

Looking ahead he saw the deep saddle that marked the entrance into the valley where the Kyle property lay and immediately felt a strong current stir through him ... Almost home ... He leaned forward, touched the sorrel lightly and broke the big red horse into a gallop.

He reached the swale, halted. A long sigh slipped from his lips. It was just as he had remembered, and every bit as beautiful. Gentle, sloping hillsides and broad meadows, all covered with grass; here and there clumps of cottonwoods; the darker blur of a piñon tree

15

grove far to his left where he'd gone as a boy to gather nuts; splashes of red and yellow flowers, the gray-green of sage.

His interest quickened. To the west an irregular shaped mass filled a wide hollow. Cattle grazing in the hot sunshine. Ben smiled. His father had a pretty fair sized herd, far larger than he had expected.

He sat for a few moments debating the problem of going first to the ranch or swinging wide and having a closer look at the herd, decided finally on the latter. It would be only a little out of the way and he wanted to see just how good a condition the stock was in; prime, he would imagine, judging from the range.

Glancing backtrail instinctively, he saw no riders in sight, and then angling off toward the west, he put the sorrel into an easy lope.

There were a good five hundred head in the herd, Ben estimated, as he rode in close. All were gathered in the hollow where water seeped to the surface and formed a shallow pool. The beef had only recently been moved onto that part of the range, he saw, noting the grass was still long and showed little evidence of trampling.

A frown crossed his face as he worked in among the steers. Henry Kyle had always used a simple K as his brand; this beef all wore a Diamond H mark. Ben considered that for a minute, shrugged it off. Evidently his father had changed his brand. He peered more closely

16

at the nearest animal; perhaps it was a Diamond K—just hard to read. But he was wrong. The mark was definitely a Diamond H. Somehow Ben found this hard to accept.

A short time later he reached the point he and his father had always termed the south gate: two widely separated masses of rock that more or less formed an entrance to the level plateau where the buildings and corrals were placed. Kyle looked eagerly.

There was little change. The same long, low-running ranch house with its slanted roof; the barn—always too small; the corrals, well shed, the cabin where the occasional hired hands bunked, the half a dozen or so lesser structures. All were there as before. The only change was that they had become more weather-beaten.

Squinting, he searched the grounds eagerly, hoping to catch sight of his father, but saw no one. Oddly, the place almost appeared deserted—but that was normal. At that hour of the day Henry Kyle would be inside, out of the sun, resting. The hired help, if any, would also be taking their ease from the heat.

Spurring the sorrel to a sudden gallop, Ben reached the yard quickly. Slowing, he allowed the horse to walk in quietly, aware now of an anxiety creeping through him. The place did, indeed, look abandoned. Weeds crowded the walls of the house, the vegetable garden that had been his father's pride was a dusty, neglected square of sterile soil lying fallow

17

within a sagging wire fence.

No horses were in any of the corrals; no chickens clucked and scratched in the pen. The windows of the barn were broken and the door of the bunkhouse hung from a single hinge.

Halting at the hitchrack, Kyle dismounted. Giving the leathers a couple of turns around the crossbar, he walked slowly across the creaking boards of the porch and tried the door latch. The panel opened with a dry squeal.

'Pa?'

Ben remained still, a lean, dark man with deep-set eyes and a hard slash for a mouth, framed in the doorway's rectangle. There was no response to his call. Shifting his pistol forward, he stepped into the room.

The furniture was familiar, only now worn, broken, covered with a thick layer of dust. Alarm shot through Ben Kyle, and moving in long strides he made a hurried tour of the house, finding nothing alive except a family of field mice.

Grim, worried, he moved to the rear, checked the barn, the crew's quarters, found conditions the same; there simply was no one living on the place; apparently it had been deserted for months—perhaps years.

Returning to the sorrel he tried to puzzle it out. Ben had never given a thought to the possibility that his father could be dead, but now that idea was beginning to take form and present itself as a reality.

18

He wouldn't have heard, of course. Being on the move, such could easily happen and he would never be aware of it. But Henry Kyle dead? He couldn't make himself believe it. Something out of the ordinary would have to happen, bring it about; his pa had been a strong man, and not really old.

Could he have sold the ranch, moved into Oak Springs or some other settlement, to spend the rest of his days?

It was a possibility, although Ben found it difficult to imagine his father sitting on a porch somewhere, idly rocking away his last years. Shaking his head, he climbed onto the sorrel, sat for a time staring at the old house. Abruptly he wheeled around, struck due east for Oak Springs. There'd be someone there who could tell him what had happened.

CHAPTER FOUR

It was midafternoon when he reached town, a collection of two dozen or so structures assembled along the west bank of the Warbucket at a point where a bridge had been erected for the convenience of travelers.

Halting at the end of the wide street separating two rows of business houses, Ben gave the settlement curious appraisal. Little had changed here either, he noted: the two-storied Warbucket Hotel with its weather-bleached chairs on the porch; Carmody's—still the largest and most prosperous looking saloon; Hansen's general store; Gibson's gun shop, where he'd stood at the window as a boy and admired the fancy weapons on display behind the glass.

On beyond the north line of business houses there appeared to be more residences than before, and a room had been added to the rear of the Baptist church, lending it a sort of humped-backed look. The minister's quarters, Ben guessed. To the south, the flat roof of the Catholic church with its whitewashed cross still dominated the scatter of huts in that area commonly known as Mexican Town.

Putting the sorrel to a slow walk, he started down the street, entering the canyon of false fronts, his glance swinging from side to side touching the few persons abroad in the heat as he sought someone he knew and from whom he could get answers.

Strangers—all of them. There could be those with whom he should be acquainted, merely by that fact he was Henry Kyle's son, but which were they? He'd been young when those infrequent visits were made to the town, and he'd been away for years. It was hardly possible...

His moody thoughts came to a stop as his eyes settled on a figure leaning against the door frame of Oak Springs' jail—the sheriff. Walt

... Walt ... Kyle fumbled for the lawman's last name—Guyman. Walt Guyman. He did remember him; still squat, broad-shouldered, hair worn long beneath a flat crowned hat, full, curling moustache. Guyman had been old seven years ago. He looked no different.

Angling the sorrel to the hitchrack fronting Guyman's office, Ben pulled to a halt. Nodding to the lawman, he dismounted, tethered the red and stepped up onto the small landing.

'Pleasured to see you again, Sheriff.'

Walt Guyman's head moved slightly, his small, quiet eyes fathomless.

'Case you don't remember, I'm Ben—Henry's Kyle's son.'

'I know you,' the lawman said as if such recognition was an effort.

Ben's manner altered somewhat. Guyman had no cause to treat him as he would an unwelcome stranger, but if that was the way he felt, the blade had two edges.

'Looking for information,' he said. 'Been out to Pa's place, found it deserted. Has been for quite a spell, I'd say. Be obliged if you could tell me where I'll find him.'

Beyond Guyman, inside the office, Ben could see a second man slouched behind a desk. He was much younger, with a thick shock of blond hair and unblinking, pale blue eyes.

Guyman said, 'Over there,' and pointed toward the Baptist church.

21

Ben followed the line of his finger, frowned. 'The church?'

'Graveyard behind it,' the lawman said bluntly. 'Buried him there next your ma.'

Kyle stood in complete silence while the impact of the information had its way with him. Every man dies eventually, some young, some old, and in his time Ben had seen death in all its varied forms; but somehow he'd never associated his father with the possibility. He guessed now he had just expected Henry Kyle to live forever.

And then suspicion began to grow within him. His pa had not been an old man, always a healthy one and unusually strong.

'How'd it happen?' he asked quietly.

'How?' Guyman echoed testily. 'Why, he just up and died, that's how. Was getting along.'

Ben shook his head. 'Not old as you, Sheriff. And there was nothing wrong with him.'

'How would you know? You ain't been around these parts in a dozen years.'

'Only seven. How long ago did he die?'

Guyman stirred. 'Year and a half ago, more or less.'

The young lawman inside shook loose from his chair, crossed the room and took up a position next to the sheriff, leaning his tall frame against the opposite edge of the doorway. Kyle glanced to him and then to Guyman.

22

The older man ducked his head sideways. 'My deputy, Tom Dane.'

Dane extended his hand. 'Pleased to know you, Kyle.'

Ben nodded, returned to the subject. 'Little surprised Pa's place is still there, being empty for so long.'

'One of the ranchers is figuring to buy it when it goes up for back taxes,' Guyman said. 'Main reason why it ain't been tore down.'

Kyle gave that a few moments' thought. He had a little cash, but likely not enough to clean up an accumulation of taxes as well as get the ranch back on its feet again.

'When will that be?'

'When it goes up for sale? Law allows a man three years. You got about half that left, if you want it.'

'Want it?' Kyle echoed. 'Hell, yes, I want it! I came back here to ranch with my pa. He's dead, so I'll go it alone.'

Guyman's expression became wooden. 'My advice to you is forget it.'

Ben's resentment and dislike for the old lawman was growing steadily. 'Mind telling me why?'

'Place is in a hell of a shape, for one thing. Take a lot of hard work. And as I recollect, you ain't one to settle down, stick with a job.'

'Man can change—'

Walt Guyman shrugged impatiently. 'Maybe, but I ain't seen it happen yet. Drifters

23

are all alike.'

Ben masked his irritation with a smile. He supposed the lawman had a right to his opinions but that didn't necessarily mean he was correct in his assumption.

'We'll see,' he murmured. 'Who's been looking after Pa's herd? Like to make things right with them.'

Guyman said, 'Henry didn't have no stock when he died. Done been sold off. Fact is, he was stone broke. Friends chipped in to see him buried proper.'

Ben received that information in stunned silence. What could have happened to Henry Kyle while he was away? None of it sounded right. But in seven years...

'Something else I'll be wanting to do—pay them back.'

'Ain't no need. Be none of them willing to take your money. Henry had a few friends.'

Kyle nodded. 'Just the same, I'll do my thanking.' He paused. 'Whose herd is that on my range? Cattle had a Diamond H brand.'

'Diamond H—that's the Halverson outfit,' Tom Dane volunteered, speaking up for the first time since being introduced.

Halverson! Ben grinned tightly. Seemed he and the red-haired rancher were slated to cross trails again. He shrugged.

'Makes no difference who it belongs to. I want my range cleared quick.'

Walt Guyman straightened slowly. 'Give

24

you a little more advice,' he said quietly; 'some you'd best take. Park Halverson's a bad man to buck. Don't push your—'

'He's already been bucked,' Ben said.

The lawman's brows drew together. 'You been to see him?'

'Run into him and his boy. And two others—one named Dave Zuda and another one they called Lonnie.'

'Lonnie Rand,' Dane said. 'Sidekick of Bud's. Always together.'

Guyman waited patiently until the deputy had finished. Then, 'You have trouble with Halverson?'

'Nothing special. Tried to keep me off Red Rye Flat. Didn't work out that way.'

Tom Dane stepped out onto the landing, lips pulled to a broad smile. 'What happened?'

'Halverson had some ideas about Bud giving me a working over. Little slip-up. I left them walking across the Flat after their horses.'

'You took their horses away from them—all four of them?' the deputy asked incredulously. 'Put them afoot?'

'Way it was—'

'Wonder you didn't get shot up!'

Ben shifted. 'Had their guns, too.'

Dane laughed, wagged his head. 'That must have sure been something! I'd give a pretty penny to have been there, seen the look on Park Halverson's face. Dave Zuda's, too.'

Walt Guyman saw no humor in the incident.

25

He glared angrily at Ben. 'Expect you've bought yourself trouble, mister—and plenty of it. Halverson's big shakes around here. Gets most anything he takes a notion he wants.'

'One way or another,' Dane finished, dryly.

'Beside the point,' the old lawman snapped, and turned to Kyle. 'You forget about your pa's place, move on.'

'Not a chance,' Ben said. 'I'm staying—and you can do me a favor. Get word to Halverson that I want his stock off my land before the week's out.'

Guyman looked down. A long sigh escaped his lips and he shrugged wearily. 'All right. I reckon it's your funeral. I'll ride over to Halverson's—'

'No need,' Dane broke in, his voice lifting slightly. 'He can tell Park himself. He's coming now.'

CHAPTER FIVE

Kyle wheeled slowly. Park Halverson, flanked by Bud, Lonnie Rand and Zuda, was just turning into the street. They rode abreast, taking up the entire width. Arrogance rode the rancher's wide shoulders like a cold-eyed eagle, and contempt for all about him seeped from the man in an almost visible cloud.

Ben saw him stiffen and his head snap back

26

when his glance halted on the landing fronting the sheriff's office. Halverson said something from the corner of his mouth to Bud, and then all four veered from their dead center path, slanted toward the jail.

'There'll be no shooting,' Walt Guyman warned in a low voice.

Kyle's jaw tightened. 'Tell him,' he said, and stepped off the landing into the loose dust.

As earlier, the four riders spread slightly, moved in to form a half circle. Ben eyed Halverson with faint scorn.

'Keep them together, Red. I get nervous when I'm hemmed in.'

Temper sent a rush of blood flooding into Park Halverson's neck and on upward into his cheeks. He jerked the black savagely to a halt.

'I'll damn well do—'

'Before you get wound up on that,' Kyle broke in coolly, 'I've got something to say. I'm giving you notice here and now: get your cattle off my range or expect some losses.'

'Why, you goddammed saddle tramp, I'll—'

Ben partly turned his head to Guyman. 'You heard me, Sheriff—you, too, Deputy. You're witnesses. I asked Halverson to get his beef off my land. Asked him peaceable. If they're not gone by the end of the week, I'll move them myself.'

Park Halverson, squirming with rage, brushed at his sweating face. 'You—you talk to me like that? Who the hell you think you

27

are?'

'I'm the man who owns the grass your beef's eating up. I want it stopped. Fact is, I may just decide to hang onto few—payment for grazing.'

'You touch one of my cows and I'll—'

Ben Kyle leaned forward gently. He was doing his talking to the rancher but his attention was on Dave Zuda.

'You'll do what, Mr Halverson?'

The big redhead hung stiff on the saddle, eyes glowing. He shot a quick glance to Zuda, to the lawmen standing behind Kyle, and then he shrugged.

'Just don't you lay a hand on none of my cows,' he said in a low voice.

'Up to you,' Ben said. 'Expect I'm within my rights to do some collecting.' He paused, added, 'That so, Sheriff?'

Guyman shook his head. 'Leave me out of this.'

Dave Zuda stirred carefully on his horse. 'You aiming to work your pa's place?'

'What I figure to do.'

'Alone?'

'Expect I can find some hands.'

'Not around here!' Halverson snapped.

Ben gave him a half smile. 'Plenty of other towns.'

'And there ain't nobody around here who'll sell you beef,' the rancher added. 'Leastwise, they better not.'

28

Impatience prodded Ben. For a man up in years Halverson had a lot to learn. 'We got everything clear?'

The rancher made no reply. Zuda finally said, 'Reckon so.'

'Good enough,' Kyle said and turned onto the landing. When he halted beside the lawmen and looked over his shoulder, Halverson and his party had pulled away and were moving down the street.

'Wait'll it gets around that somebody backed Park Halverson off,' the deputy said, grinning. 'And if it ever gets out you set him and them others afoot, made them hoof it across—'

'Be enough of that!' Walt Guyman cut in sharply.

Dane sobered and a quick anger filled his eyes. 'Better get used to it, Sheriff,' he said. 'Things are changing around here. The old days are gone.'

The lawman gave his deputy a bitter look. 'And I ain't big enough for the job no more— that what you're saying?'

'You're saying it, not me,' Dane replied and stepped back into the office.

Walt Guyman brushed irritably at his moustache, swung his attention to Kyle. 'And you—you're a bigger damn fool than I thought!'

'Why? Because I want what's mine?'

'Goes deeper than that. You don't shove a

29

man like Park Halverson around.'

'Seems to me all the shoving's being done by him.'

Guyman cocked his head, spat. 'All in how you look at it. Anyway, that grass was going to waste. If he hadn't used it, somebody else would.'

'Not denying that,' Ben retorted. The lawman's defense of Halverson was rubbing him wrong. 'But now I want it stopped. Be making use of it myself.'

Guyman's lips cracked into a thin smile. 'You sure that's what you've got in mind—or you just using that as an excuse?'

'Excuse for what?'

'Halverson's a big man. Wouldn't be the first time some gunnie purposely picked a fight with his kind just to prove how good he was.'

'Wrong, Sheriff,' Kyle said. 'Seen all the trouble I want. All I'm looking for is peace and quiet.'

Nodding curtly, Ben moved on down the walk, pointing for Hansen's. There was no sense returning to the ranch for the night, he had decided. It was growing late and much had to be done to the house before accommodations would be suitable. Best idea was to stay at the hotel and head back early in the morning. It would take two, possibly three days to put things in order, and by then Halverson would have his herd moved ... if he intended to do so.

Reaching Hansen's porch, he crossed and entered, faced the storekeeper, who regarded him with cool reserve, giving no sign of recognition. Ignoring the man's obvious reluctance, Kyle placed an order for the food he figured necessary to last him for a while.

Finished, he paid the bill, said, 'Be obliged if you'll dump all that in a couple of flour sacks. Be by in the morning after it.'

'Sure,' Hansen said with no show of interest. 'Door's open at six o'clock.'

'You know the name?'

The storekeeper bobbed his balding head. 'I know,' he murmured.

Ben spun on his heel, returned to the porch. He stood for a minute in the late afternoon's heat, idly thinking over Hansen's attitude. Others in Oak Springs would feel the same—would actually hate him because he was a threat and was placing their relationship with Park Halverson in jeopardy. Like Walt Guyman they wanted nothing to upset the delicate balance; they preferred to tread softly, turn their backs on the rancher's ruthless activities, and pretend all was well.

A bleak smile crossed his lips. Tom Dane had said it in so many words, all to the point: *the old days were gone.* And they were insofar as Ben Kyle and Halverson were concerned— not that he felt he should lead a crusade to challenge and pull down the big rancher—but simply because what was his, was his, and he intended to keep it.

Wheeling, he retraced his steps to the hitchrack in front of Guyman's office. The old lawman was no longer around but Dane glanced up from the desk, gave him a brief nod as he swung to the saddle and headed back up the street for the Warbucket Hotel.

He rode first to the stable behind the tall structure, maintained for use of the paying guests, entered the wide doorway, and dismounted. An aged hostler with a tobacco-stained beard shuffled out of the deep shadows, greeted him with a nod.

Ben said, 'Want him rubbed down and grain fed, then watered. You be doing it or will it be somebody else?'

The old man splattered brown juice against a post. 'Seeing as how I'm the only one working here, I reckon it'll be me.'

Kyle reached into his pocket for a coin. 'Have him saddled and ready to go by daylight.'

The hostler accepted the coin, glanced at it, grinned. 'Sure thing, mister. Be just like you're saying.'

Ben turned away, entered the hotel by its rear door. Registering, he went immediately to his room, stripped and washed down, using the china bowl and pitcher. He'd left his change of clothing in his saddlebags, decided going after them wasn't worth the effort. And he could get by another day without a shave. Crawling onto the bed, he fell asleep at once.

When he awoke it was full dark and the street below was aglow with lamps from the stores' windows. Dressing leisurely, he went downstairs, paused at the desk.

'Man's wanting a good steak where does he go?'

The clerk, little more than a boy, pointed to a door at the opposite end of the lobby.

'Got our own restaurant in there. Folks around here claim it's the best.'

It was a good meal served in quiet surroundings; when it was over and Ben was again on the sidewalk he felt much better. The nap had washed all desire for sleep from him now and he turned his attention to the lower end of the street where Carmody's saloon, bright with lights and issuing sounds of piano music, was drawing a crowd.

Coming to a quick decision, he stepped down into the dust, finding it easier walking than the board sidewalk, and struck for Carmody's. A couple of drinks, perhaps a turn or two at cards and then maybe he'd feel like bed. Be good to have a little fun, anyway; he could see nothing ahead at the ranch but a lot of hard work.

The ranch ... That brought to mind his father. Before he rode out in the morning, he'd drop by the church, thank the minister for what he'd done and find out who the friends were that had pitched in on the funeral. He

33

wanted to visit the graves, too, see that they were being properly attended to.

He pushed through the batwings of Carmody's, paused momentarily in the glare, and then crossed to the bar. The place was crowded and it was necessary to elbow his way up to the counter.

'Whiskey,' he said to the bartender, dropping a coin.

The aproned man reached for a bottle and glass, poured, mumbled his thanks. Kyle took up his drink. Turning lazily, he hooked his elbows on the edge of the bar and looked out over the smoke-filled room.

Sitting at a table directly opposite were Bud Halverson and Lonnie Rand.

CHAPTER SIX

Kyle returned the sullen stares of the two men, allowed his glance to drift on. Likely Halverson and Dave Zuda were around also, but he did not see them. In one of the back rooms, probably, not that it mattered. He'd had his say and that was the end of it unless Diamond H stock still grazed on his range when the deadline was up.

Sipping at the strong liquor, he brought his attention to a stop on a card game underway in a far corner of the saloon. Five men surrounded the circular table but only four were holding cards, the odd member apparently having dropped out and now simply watching.

Ben tossed off the last of his drink, set the shot glass on the bar. He'd try a few hands of five-card stud, then ... He drew up stiffly, feeling the hard, round press of a six-gun's muzzle against his side. Kyle came around slowly. Lonnie Rand, pistol hidden by his own body, was crowding in close. In front, mouth sagging weakly, eyes abnormally bright, was Bud Halverson.

'We're going outside,' Bud said thickly. 'Got a little unfinished business Pa's expecting me to take care of.'

'Don't try nothing cute,' Rand warned in a low voice. 'Just head for the door.'

Ben forced a bleak smile. 'You're both drunk. Get the hell away and leave me be.'

A man standing to Kyle's left turned inquiringly, features pulled into a puzzled frown. Abruptly the look faded and he drew away hurriedly. Others nearby took note and in only moments Kyle, Halverson and Rand were alone in the center of a cleared space in the hushed saloon.

Bud shifted nervously on his feet, swallowed hard, but Rand remained fixed, maintaining steady pressure with the pistol against Ben's ribs.

'You hear?' he said hoarsely. 'Start walking.'

35

Halverson, taking courage from Lonnie Rand's refusal to back off, glanced around, moved a half step nearer to Ben.

'All right, mister, you want it here, you'll get it. All the same to me.'

'Forget, it Bud,' Kyle said. 'I don't want any trouble with you.'

'You got it anyway. Nobody pushes a Halverson—'

'That's your pa talking,' Ben cut in, 'not you. Why don't you grow up, start being your own man!'

Bud flushed. Rand dug his gun barrel deeper into Kyle's ribs. Ben flinched, began to turn slowly.

'Get his gun!' Halverson shouted in a strangled voice at Rand. 'This jasper's going to learn who's who around here!'

Kyle felt weight lessen on his hip as Lonnie plucked his pistol from its holster. All humor and patience deserted him in that moment, and a dull anger began to rise. It was easy to see what the pair had in mind: Lonnie would keep him pinned against the bar under the threat of his weapon while Bud used his fists. He faced Halverson coolly.

'Back off. My quarrel's with your pa.'

'Makes no difference!' Bud yelled and swung a wild right.

Kyle dodged easily, but trapped against the bar he was unable to avoid the awkward blow entirely, took a glancing rap on the shoulder.

36

Seizing Halverson's wrist, he spun the man about, shoved him stumbling into the first row of tables and chairs.

A yell went up in the saloon. The bartender began to shout and Kyle realized that if Park Halverson and Zuda were somewhere on the premises the commotion would summon them. And against the four...

'Stay right where you are,' Rand ordered. 'I'd as soon pull this trigger as not.'

Kyle swept the room with a searching glance, came back to Lonnie. There had been no sign of the elder Halverson and his gunman sidekick.

'You right sure you want in on this?'

Lonnie nodded. 'Damn sure.'

Bud Halverson, on his feet, head seemingly much clearer, was advancing warily. The grin had left his face and he now wore a look of desperate determination. Men in the room began to speak up, encourage Bud to wade right in, finish the job he'd started, teach the drifter who the Halversons were.

Kyle watched Bud narrowly. He could do little, backed against the counter; he must somehow rid himself of Lonnie and the threat of the pistol in the rider's hand. As long as he was thus trapped he could only hope to avoid Bud's blows and offer little retaliation, but he'd not get away with that for long; sooner or later Bud would get lucky. One thing was in his favor: Park Halverson and Zuda evidently

37

weren't in the saloon. That evened the odds a little. He winced again as Rand stabbed him with the gun barrel, and then a tight grin broke the line of his mouth.

Settling forward, body loose, Ben watched as Bud, first taking a sharp look to be certain Lonnie still held his gun, closed in. He saw the blow coming, intentionally failed to dodge, took it on the side of the head. The force of it rocked him slightly but did no particular damage, but did serve his purpose.

Grunting, he sagged forward, went to his knees. A shout went up and he felt Lonnie Rand's pistol jerk from his side, saw the young man step back.

'Get him, Bud! Get him now!'

Ben Kyle came upright and whirled in a single, flowing motion. His balled fist lashed out. It caught Rand on the side of the jaw, dropped him flat.

Spinning, he took Bud Halverson's wild rush straight on. The weight of the man carried him crashing against the bar, setting up a clatter of glass. He fought to hold his footing, flinching under the blows Bud was raining on his neck and head.

Anger was boiling through him now in a towering wave and what little pity and sympathy he had felt for Park Halverson's browbeaten son had vanished. If he went down, Bud, in his desperate hope of living up to his father's expectations, would show him no mercy ... And if too many moments slipped by Lonnie Rand would regain his senses and he would have him to reckon with again.

Ben, his feet finally freed of their entanglement with the bar rail, set himself squarely. Halverson was clinging tight to him, one arm wrapped around his body; with the other he was flailing away, endeavoring to land an effective blow. The bartender was yelling something and above the steady din in the room a woman's voice was screaming.

Kyle buckled forward, using the counter as leverage, and made room for his own arms. Doubling his right fist, he drove it deep into Halverson's belly. Bud gasped with pain, loosened his grip. Ben struck again, this time with a sharp left followed quickly by a right. Halverson broke clear, staggered back, mouth gaped wide as he sucked for air.

Kyle hit him hard and clean on the chin. Bud staggered, began to twist slowly. Ben closed fast, smashed another hard blow to the head. Halverson stumbled away, fell against one of the overturned tables.

Breathing hard from his own efforts, Ben swung to Rand. Lonnie was pulling himself to his feet, his movements loose and uncertain, his head hanging forward. Through slowly clearing eyes he saw his pistol on the floor near his feet, made an unsteady grab for it.

Kyle crossed quickly, kicked the weapon, sent it skittering into a far corner of the saloon.

39

Seizing Rand by the shirtfront, he jerked the man upright, swung him around, threw him at Halverson sprawled against the shattered table.

In the splintering sound that followed Kyle dropped back a step, recovered his own pistol from the bar where Lonnie had placed it, jammed it into its holster. He stood for a long moment staring at the hushed crowd and then turned to the counter.

'Another whiskey.'

The bartender, his features solemn, complied hurriedly. Placing the glass before Ben he leaned forward.

'Was I you, friend, I'd get out of this town fast. Park Halverson ain't going to take kindly to your working over his boy.'

Kyle downed his liquor, nodded. Anger was still having its strong way with him and his jaw was set.

'The hell with Park Halverson,' he snapped. 'He sends somebody to jump me again I'll do more than work them over.'

Wheeling, he stalked through the crowd and into the street. He was no longer in any mood for five-card stud.

CHAPTER SEVEN

Hammering on his door woke Ben Kyle from a sound sleep. He sat up, shook his head to clear the cobwebs.

'Kyle! Open up!'

Ben reached for his pants, drew them on. It was Walt Guyman's voice. He swore softly as he strapped on his gunbelt.

'Kyle!'

'What do you want?' he shouted, stalling until he could complete dressing.

'Open the door. It's Guyman—the sheriff.'

Ben delayed another minute, then crossed to the flimsy panel and turned the key. Stepping back, he said, 'It's open.'

The door swung in. Guyman, pistol drawn, entered slowly. Following closely were Park Halverson and Dave Zuda. Kyle leaned against the wall, studied the rancher coldly.

'You're a hard loser, Red.'

Halverson's eyes flamed. 'You goddammed murdering tramp!' he shouted and lurched forward.

Kyle's hand dropped to the butt of his pistol. Guyman flung up an arm, checked the rancher, scowled at Dave Zuda, suddenly on the far side of the room.

'Be none of that!' he barked, pushing Halverson back. Pointing at Ben's weapon, he

41

added, 'Forget it. You're under arrest.'

Kyle's eyes were on the rancher, his mind stuck dead center on the words he had shouted. 'What's this all about?'

'Don't be trying to pull that!' the rancher said, curling his lips. 'You know the answer.'

'You sent your kid and his sidekick to give me a working over and it didn't turn out that way. Know that much.'

'I'm jailing you for murder,' Guyman said quietly. 'Raise your hands.'

Ben stared. 'Murder!' he echoed. 'What kind of raw deal is this?'

'Nothing raw about it. Bud Halverson's dead—beat to death.'

Kyle's glance shifted to Halverson, to Zuda, obviously guarding the window, back to the lawman. 'You figure I did it?'

'Looks that way,' Guyman said, moving in and relieving Kyle of his pistol. 'You want to talk about it, we'll do it in my jail.'

It was barely daylight as the four men came from the Warbucket Hotel and entered the street. No one was abroad at that early hour and they reached the jail unseen. Guyman conducted Kyle to the single, empty cell, slammed and locked the door. Tossing the keys onto his desk, he settled on one corner.

'You got some talking to do, now's the time,' he said.

'What's the point in listening to him?' Park Halverson broke in impatiently. 'We know he done it. So's everybody else.'

'Everybody else—and you—are wrong,' Ben said flatly. 'If Bud's dead I had nothing to do with it.'

Halverson pressed forward angrily. 'You saying there wasn't no fight in Carmody's last night?'

'Not saying that, but Bud was a long way from being dead when I walked out. Knocked cold—him and Lonnie Rand both—but that was all.'

'And you denying you told Pete Evans you'd kill Bud if he caused you any more trouble?'

'Evans?'

'Carmody's bartender,' Guyman said. 'Told us you were talking to him when it was all over.'

'Never said anything about a killing. Was plenty riled, I'll admit.'

'So Evans claimed. Way it looks to me, Bud and Lonnie Rand followed you out of the saloon—'

'Weren't in any shape to follow me.'

'Well, you waited outside till they did, started the ruckus all over again. Only this time you didn't stop when he was down. You kept at him, killed him.'

'You're wrong, Sheriff,' Kyle said in disgust. 'Nothing like that at all. I went straight to the hotel, crawled in bed. Wasn't out of the room until you came after me.'

'You prove that?'

Kyle shook his head. He could recall seeing no one on the street or in the lobby of the hotel. And he had slept soundly.

'No way I can think of. However, law says you'll have to prove I didn't do what I said.'

Immediately Park Halverson turned, drew Zuda to one side, began to speak to the man in a low, rapid voice.

'Your story ain't worth much,' the lawman said, getting to his feet. 'Better be digging up some witnesses.'

Ben brought his attention back to Guyman. 'Man goes to bed, falls asleep. How's he going to know if he had a witness to that?'

'You'll be needing a couple, just the same,' Guyman said with a shrug. 'Facts are pretty plain.'

'What facts? You don't have any and you know it. Who found Bud and where?'

'His pa found him. Zuda and him come looking for the boy, run across him in that alleyway alongside Carmody's.'

'Lonnie Rand there, too?'

The sheriff nodded. 'Been knocked cold.'

'And I'm supposed to've done it—beat up both of them, killed Bud?'

'You're the one having trouble with them and the one making the threats.'

'Was no threat,' Ben said doggedly. He paused, watched Zuda slip silently through the doorway, disappear into the street. 'Maybe sounded like it, but it wasn't.'

44

'Everybody figures it was. And you had other reasons ... that run-in you and the Halversons had earlier in the day. And him grazing cattle on your range. Sounds to me like you seen a chance to get even, grabbed it.'

Kyle sighed gustily. 'Maybe seems that way to you, Sheriff but you're wrong. You aim to hold me? You got to have some kind of proof to do that.'

'Got motive,' Guyman said calmly. 'Figure that's enough. Anything more you want to say?'

Halverson had turned from the door, was sitting now on the corner of Guyman's desk, his small, hard eyes drilling into Ben Kyle with relentless intensity. There was little grief visible in his manner, only a sullen vindictiveness.

'There a lawyer in this town?'

Guyman said, 'A couple. Doubt if either one'll be much interested in helping you.'

'Want to talk to them, anyway.'

'Don't waste your time,' Halverson said dryly. 'I got you dead to rights. You'll be swinging from a rope before—'

'I've got the prisoner,' Guyman cut in icily. 'And as for hanging, the judge'll decide that after a jury's had its say.' The lawman turned completely around, faced Halverson. 'Want you to get that straight, Park. I'll stand for no foolishness.'

The big rancher lifted his hands, allowed them to fall. 'Sure, sure, Walt! All I'm asking is

45

justice for my dead boy.'

'Boy,' Guyman grunted. 'He was twenty-three years old, I figure, and knew what things was all about. He'll get justice.'

'All I want. How long'll we have to wait for that judge to get here?'

'Not due for a couple of weeks. Maybe could get him sooner by writing a letter.'

Halverson rose, rubbing his huge hands together. 'Expect you'd better do that, Walt. Can't be responsible for what folks around here'll do once word gets out about the murder.'

'I can handle the people in town,' Guyman said, jerking open a drawer of his desk and dropping Ben's pistol into it. 'You just see that your bunch behaves.'

The rancher wagged his head. 'It'll be sort of touchy. Boys all thought a lot of Bud, but I'll be doing my best.'

'You do more'n that. I plain don't know if Kyle here's guilty or not. Up to the judge and jury to figure that. Up to me to see he stays alive long enough to stand trial.'

The rancher turned toward the door. Halfway he hesitated, glanced back. 'Your job, I know that, but you know something else, Walt? Right now I sure would hate to be walking in your boots.'

Guyman watched Halverson step out into the street, point for Carmody's. He remained there, staring into the brightening light for a

46

full minute, then came slowly, wearily around.

'Be sending you over some breakfast soon as the restaurant opens,' he said. 'Anything else you're needing?'

Kyle settled back on his hard cot. 'Luck. Sounds like I'm needing that most.'

'I aim to talk to Evans, the bartender, again. Maybe ask some questions of some others. Might be I'll turn up a couple of things that'll help.'

'That mean you don't think I did it?'

Walt Guyman moved toward the doorway. 'Like I told Halverson, not up to me to do no thinking. My job's to lock you up, keep you ready for a trial. Judge does all the rest.'

'Don't have much money on me, Sheriff, but there any chance for bail? Be hard for me to find any witnesses locked up in a cell.'

'Won't need to look; I'll do it for you,' Guyman said and pulled the door closed as he walked out.

A moment later Ben heard a key turn in the lock. He stared at the door moodily. It would be some protection but not enough if Park Halverson and his crew decided to take the law into their own hands. And that was what the rancher had in mind, he was certain. The quiet conversation between him and Dave Zuda gave every indication of such. Likely...

The door at the end of the narrow corridor to the rear of the jail rattled faintly. Rising, Ben pressed himself against the bars for a better view. He heard a click, and then light splashed across the shadowy hall. Boot heels rapped hollowly on the bare floor.

A moment later Tom Dane strode by, eyes straight ahead. He passed Kyle unseeing, crossed the small quarters and took up a broom standing in the corner beyond Walt Guyman's desk. Wheeling, he retraced his steps, pausing only long enough to lean the broom against the bars of Kyle's cell.

Ben watched the deputy in amazement. 'What—?'

'You ain't seen me,' Dane said, brushing on by and entering the corridor. 'Understand? You ain't seen me.'

CHAPTER EIGHT

Kyle listened to the door close, waited for the dry snap of the lock. It did not come. He stood for several moments pondering the deputy's strange behavior. Why would Tom Dane want him to escape? He could find no answer and, turning away, reached for the broom. Ben Kyle only knew a route to freedom was open and he'd best take advantage of it.

Holding the end of the broom handle in both hands, he raked the ring of keys off Guyman's desk. It was a simple matter to drag them within reach. Selecting the proper key, he

48

inserted it in the cell door lock. The grille opened with the first twist.

Again Kyle hesitated, suspicious and unwilling to accept the benefaction dropped into his lap. Dane must have an angle, a reason; no deputy would simply walk in, intentionally make it possible for an accused murderer to escape, and then walk out.

Was it that Tom Dane, lying in wait outside, wanted him to make a run for it so that he could shoot him down as he fled?

That was it. Either the deputy, who had given Ben the impression that he would like very much to wear Walt Guyman's sheriff badge, was seeking glory and the furtherance of that ambition by halting a jailbreaker, or he was working for Park Halverson. It had to be one or the other.

Kyle grinned tightly, stepped from his cell into the center of the office. Two could play at that game; if Tom Dane expected him to come rushing out the back door, conveniently left unlocked, he was due for a surprise.

Crossing hurriedly to Guyman's desk, Kyle recovered his pistol, dropped it into place. Then taking the ring of keys, he sorted through the half dozen or so until he found the one that fitted the front entrance. Releasing the tumblers, he opened the panel a narrow crack and surveyed the street.

Two men lounged in the battered chairs on the veranda of the Warbucket Hotel, almost directly across. Farther down the way a lone rider, slumped on the saddle, was turning into Carmody's hitchrack. A sunbonneted woman in housedress and apron was probing about in the stock of tubs and water buckets piled on the porch fronting Hansen's store, to his left.

He swore softly. In order to reach the stable behind the hotel where he had quartered his horse, he would have to cross the street. Such was certain to draw the attention of the men on the veranda. And Walt Guyman, somewhere among the stores, could put in an appearance at any moment.

To go out the back way would be simple. He'd come out behind the stores on the south side of the street, and while it would still be necessary to cross, he could drop to the extreme end of the row of structures, where there were residences, and then move to the opposite side. Possibilities of being noticed at that far distance from the center of town were small—but the chances were good he'd be playing right into Tom Dane's hands.

He had no choice. Glancing about, he spotted a worn brush jacket—Guyman's or Tom Dane's—hanging from a peg behind the desk. It offered some degree of disguise. Pulling it on he returned to the door, again studied the street. The woman had disappeared, likely was inside Hansen's completing her purchasing. Only the horse was now in front of Carmody's saloon, and the two men on the Warbucket's porch were in deep conversation, both half turned from him. No one else was in sight.

Quiet, he slipped out onto the landing fronting the jail, and moving with repressed deliberation—a man leisurely carrying out an unimportant errand—he cut left, skirted Hansen's and stepped up onto the walk. The pair across the street glanced up, touched him briefly and disinterestedly with their eyes, resumed their conversation.

Taut, Kyle continued along the walk for the necessary distance, moved off the planks into the dust, and crossed over, his shuttered gaze whipping back and forth along the fronts of the store buildings.

Reaching the corner of the hotel, he breathed easier. No one had taken notice of him, other than the two men in front of the Warbucket, and he doubted if his appearance had registered on their minds.

He broke into a trot, heading for the stable at the rear of the hostelry, hoping the wrangler had not forgotten his instructions to have the sorrel ready. He wanted to spend no more time in Oak Springs than absolutely necessary.

Reaching the broad, low-roofed building, he ducked inside. The sorrel was standing in the runway waiting. Kyle heaved another sigh, jerked the reins loose.

'Been standing there a hour!' a voice called from the depths of the barn.

51

Ben jumped slightly at the unexpected sound, recovered. 'Obliged to you,' he answered, swinging to the saddle. 'Owe you anything?'

'Nope, reckon not.'

Kyle touched the brim of his hat and cut back to the front of the building. His best chances lay in the hills to the west, he reasoned. Immediately he put the big red into motion and struck off in that direction, thankful for the many sheds and outhouses that shielded him from the street a hundred yards to his left.

A gunshot rapped hollowly through the morning hush.

Kyle, just beyond the last of the houses, pulled up abruptly. Tom Dane's shout, loud and distinct, coming from somewhere near the jail, reached him.

'Jailbreak! Pris'ner's escaped! Anybody seen the sheriff?'

Ben tarried no longer. Digging spurs into the sorrel, he broke clear of the settlement and raced for the distant hills at a hard gallop. Almost instantly a yell went up from a corral behind him.

'There he goes!'

Kyle cursed savagely. He'd almost gotten away clean. If Tom Dane had waited only a minute more...

But it was too late to think about that. He must reach the rough country on the far side of Red Rye Flat before a posse could get lined up and on his trail. Once there he could find ample hiding places, lie low until he could decide what had to be done.

That point was clear; it was up to him to find Bud Halverson's killer.

He had no trail supplies. Ben realized that a moment later. The grub he'd ordered and paid for was still waiting for him at Hansen's. As well forget it—returning would be no less than putting a rope around his neck. They'd all figure him guilty now, making a break as he had.

But let them think it. He was up against a marked deck where Halverson was concerned. And locked in a cell he was helpless. His one hope was to ferret out Bud's murderer and turn him over to Walt Guyman.

Or Tom Dane.

He gave that thought, shook his head. He couldn't figure out the deputy, consequently was finding it hard to trust him. The reason for Dane's permitting him to escape was still a puzzle, and because of that he could put no faith in the man. One thing was sure. Tom Dane had been near the jail; his raising an alarm proved that.

Ben grinned faintly. If Tom had been planning on a big grandstand play, recapturing him as he made an escape, things had certainly gone wrong for the deputy. Kyle was almost sorry for him—almost, but not really.

He glanced back, felt his nerves tighten. Half

53

a dozen riders were breaking from the scatter of houses, lining out in his wake. It hadn't taken long to get a posse into motion. He swung his attention to the hills ahead. They were some distance away, but to his left a stand of trees forming a rim along the edge of the Flat offered concealment.

Immediately he veered the sorrel toward that point, hoping he had not yet been seen by the riders. If they were forced to depend on tracking him, their approach would be much slower. He reached the grove, and the big red, beginning to heave from the hard, fast run, slackened his pace.

At that moment Ben Kyle heard voices and drew to a quick halt. The sounds came from his left. Touching the sorrel lightly, he guided him into a pocket of dense brush, once more stopped. Raising himself in the stirrups, he peered through the shadows.

It was Park Halverson, Zuda and several Diamond H riders. He settled back, listened to their passing, wishing he could hear what was being said. But Ben Kyle had a good idea of what it was all about.

The rancher was not waiting for the judge. His words and attitude when he had been in the sheriff's office speaking with Walt Guyman, his quiet talk with Dave Zuda, and then the gunman's silent departure, made his intentions clear.

He'd got out of Oak Springs just in time, Ben

thought grimly, but now his problems had increased. The Diamond H party would unite with the posse, more than doubling its size, and together they would comb the hills. Keeping clear of them was going to be hard.

CHAPTER NINE

A time later Ben Kyle halted at the end of the grove. Ahead of him, five miles distant, lay the foothills of the mountains—with nothing between but open country.

He twisted about, glancing over his shoulder. There was no sign of the posse as yet, but by then the two factions would have met, joined and now be on his trail. Screened by the trees he had not been visible to them, just as they were blocked from his view.

That mattered little. They were aware of the direction he had taken, and in a broad land notable for its empty spaces, he could not hope to find substantial cover until he gained the brushy slopes and rugged canyons of the Sage Mountains. Eventually he would be seen.

He sat quiet in the shadows debating his best move, sullenly angered at being forced to seek hiding. It was dangerous to remain in the grove and hope the posse would pass him by. With so many in the party one was certain to see him.

He could swing south, but again he would

55

quickly break out onto open land. Areas to the north and east offered no better. Only to the west, where the towering Sages etched their smoky outline against the sky, could he expect to find a measure of safety. He'd be wise to stick to his original plan.

Coming to that decision, he roweled the sorrel out of the grove, broke onto the plain at a strong lope. At once he heard the distant, flat slap of a gunshot, threw a hasty look to the rear.

He had been spotted by one of the riders who had announced his discovery by firing a pistol. Only that member of the posse, riding well outside the trees, was in view. The others, Ben guessed, were scattered through the grove.

It changed nothing. He'd expected to be seen once beyond the screen of shrubbery; he'd only hoped to be nearer to the mountains when that moment came. Now his lead on the posse would be decreased and the time for losing himself in the hills would be shortened.

He urged the sorrel to a faster pace. Riders were beginning to stream from the grove, all drawing together into a tighter group now that their objective had been located. Ben had no difficulty singling out Park Halverson on his long-legged black horse. The man close by the rancher was Walt Guyman, he thought, but was not sure; it could be Dave Zuda.

The first rocky outcrop, with its gradual rise in the trail, drew nearer, and shortly he was within the scatter of boulders and loose shale marking the base of the mountains, and beginning the ascent. Again he looked back, felt a spurt of surprise. The posse had gained perceptibly. Halverson was driving hard. It would be the rancher, he knew, and not Guyman, pressing them on.

Suddenly the sorrel stumbled, caught himself, began to limp. Worry rushed through Ben Kyle ... A lame horse—with the posse closing in ... He looked ahead anxiously. He was just above the rock slides, beginning to enter the timbered area of the slope gashed on one side by many small, brush-filled canyons. If he could find one large enough and sufficiently overgrown...

Somewhere down slope at the foot of the trail a voice shouted something but the words were lost in the distance to Ben. The sorrel, favoring his right foreleg, drew abreast a fairly wide wash. Immediately Kyle swung off into its brush-choked mouth, relieved that the rocky surface of the trail would betray no tracks.

He dropped from the saddle, moved out in front of the sorrel, began to bull his way through the tangled growth. Passage was noisy but there was no time to use care, and he was fairly sure the riders were still far enough down the slope not to hear.

He pushed on, fighting the scrubby junipers, the tough clumps of buckbriar for a full fifty yards and then halted. Turning, he listened.

The steady thud of hooves on the trail was plain and sounded much closer in the clear air than it actually was. He wheeled then to the sorrel, thumped the red's leg until he raised it. A sigh of relief escaped Ben Kyle. It was only a small pebble wedged in the hoof. Being there for so short a time it likely had not even bruised the foot. Picking up a small stick, he flipped it loose.

He heard voices. The posse was passing the mouth of the canyon where he had sought refuge. Standing absolutely motionless, he waited while the party rode by. Finally, when he could hear only muffled thumps and an occasional click of a metal shoe against rock, he relaxed, wiped at the sweat gathered on his brow. It had been close.

Turning, he looked up the canyon, wondered if there was a possibility of exit at that end. A palisade of frowning granite studded with gnarled, sparsely leafed oak bushes rose before him in the near distance. A box canyon. The only way out was to retrace his path to the trail.

Still leading the sorrel, he began to double back the way he had come. Drawing near the entrance to the wash, he halted and, ground reining the red, moved forward cautiously to the edge of the brush. There was no one in sight; the posse was well above him, somewhere on the slope.

Dropping back to the sorrel, Ben led him quickly from the brush and stepped to the saddle. Heading down trail, he put the horse to a fast walk, not wanting to risk the echoes of a lope that might possibly draw the attention of the men in the distance.

Where now?

He pondered that problem. His intentions had been to hide somewhere on the mountain but the posse's unexpectedly fast arrival coupled with the sorrel's temporary lameness precluded that. Halverson, in effect, had beaten him to the mountain, and he and his men would search every shadow.

Ride off the slope—and keep going? He shook his head. That was no answer. He had to remain and find the killer of Bud Halverson, clear his name.

Lonnie Rand . . . .

It came to him suddenly that Lonnie was possibly the key to it all. Lonnie had been with Bud at the time of the murder, had himself, according to Halverson and Dave Zuda, also suffered a beating.

Rand would then know who Bud's assailant was, assuming he was conscious long enough to have a look. But that didn't add up, Ben realized; if Lonnie Rand actually saw the killer, Halverson would not be accusing him, would instead be demanding the blood of someone else.

Either Lonnie had purposely lied, or he had

not seen the murderer, and Kyle found the latter hard to believe. It seemed likely he would have had at least a quick glimpse.

Regardless, Lonnie Rand was the nearest thing he could look to for answers. He frowned then, thinking back to the grove a short time ago. Rand had not been in the Halverson party that later joined the posse. Such would indicate he was injured, unable to ride.

This could be a ready-made opportunity for having a talk with the young rider, Kyle decided, and wondered where he most likely could be found. Recovering from his beating at the doctor's office in Oak Springs? Or was the possibility greater that he would be at the Halverson ranch?

Odds were best that it was the ranch. Park Halverson would be the sort to look after his own, once the emergency was over. Lonnie probably was nursing his wounds in the Diamond H bunkhouse—and with the rancher and all available hired hands somewhere on the mountain, there would be no more opportune time than now to have a talk.

Ben realized in that next moment that he had no idea where Halverson's ranch lay. Somewhere to the south, he would assume, judging from the fact the rancher and his men had earlier come from that direction. But that covered a lot of ground, and he could lose a vast amount of time in aimless searching. It would be wise to head for one of the ranches he knew of, make inquiries.

He glanced beyond the sorrel. They were almost to the foot of the mountain. Twisting around, he strained for sounds of the posse returning. All was quiet. The party was still working toward the summit of the mountain. If he moved fast, determined the location of the Diamond H, there still was a good chance he could...

Kyle pulled up abruptly at the last bend in the trail. A rider, pistol drawn, blocked his way. Halverson had posted a man on guard.

'Hold it!' the puncher shouted.

Ben threw himself sideways on the saddle, drew fast. The Diamond H rider's weapon blasted and Kyle felt a searing pain lance through his left arm. He triggered his own gun as he drove spurs deep into the sorrel's flanks.

The rider yelled, grabbed for his leg, losing his weapon in the process. Kyle raced down at him, crowding him off the path, and swept by at a hard gallop. A moment later he was behind a shoulder of rock and lost to view.

But the damage was done. The gunshots would have been heard. The posse would immediately abandon its hunt on the mountainside, come hurriedly down the trail. And he was wounded.

Kyle swore angrily, holstered his gun and made a hasty examination of the bullet's effect. It had struck high on his arm, a flesh wound, but it was bleeding profusely. Allowing the sorrel to maintain a fast walk, he drew his handkerchief, wrapped it around the injury. An improvised bandage would help some, but the wound should be cleansed and properly treated.

He reached the last of the rocks, halted uncertainly. Riding all the way to Oak Springs for medical attention was out of the question.

There was a ranch to the north, he recalled. Belonged to a man named Melrose—a friend of his father's. Of course the place could have changed hands during the years, or possibly had been abandoned to Halverson, but it appeared to be his only hope.

He stirred impatiently, a light-headedness annoying him. Again he swore. Hell, he wasn't hurt that bad—nothing more than a scratch! He guessed it was caused by the loss of blood. Reaching up, he pressed the improvised bandage harder against the wound, slowing the steady drain.

He heard the hoofbeats on the trail behind him, quickly swung into a maze of rocks and rabbit-brush to his right. It would have to be the man he'd encountered; the posse wouldn't have had time to reach the point.

Two riders ... He stared at them from the brush, surprised. One was the man he'd shot, the other was Deputy Tom Dane. Understanding came to Kyle. Park Halverson or Guyman, whichever was calling the play, had apparently stationed men at various places along the slope. Dane must have been just above the canyon where he had hidden. The gunshot brought him down trail quickly.

'Headed south,' the deputy said, eyes on the loose sand beyond the rocks. 'His ranch is that way.'

'Well, I winged him for damn sure,' the Diamond H man said, holding a folded rag to the wound in his thigh. 'Probably aiming to fort up there.'

Dane nodded. 'Just what he's doing. You go back, meet the rest of the posse. Tell them that. I'll—'

'I'm bleeding like a stuck hog,' the rider complained. 'Maybe I ought to head for town.'

'Sheriff's got medicine and stuff in his saddlebags. He'll take care of you. Tell Halverson I'm following Kyle, and if he ain't making for his place, I'll leave sign for him to go by. Understand?'

The puncher bobbed his head. Immediately Tom Dane spurred away, eyes lifted as he scanned the ragged brush along the rim of the Flat. Halverson's man watched him for a time and then, swearing, wheeled about, started back up the slope to meet the posse.

Ben waited out a full minute and then moved out of the coulee. Pointing due north, he swung onto a faint trail that clung tight to the base of the mountain and thus was well hidden from the slope above. If he found no help at Melrose's—well, he'd figure something else.

63

The way he felt, one thing at a time was about all he could manage.

CHAPTER TEN

Ben Kyle rode under the pole gate crossbar and into the Melrose yard late in the morning. The spells of giddiness that had claimed him periodically during the long ride were less frequent now due probably to the fact he had covered those last miles with fingers clamped tight over his wound, preventing further loss of blood. But he was weak and he stayed on the saddle when the sorrel halted at the hitchrack.

'Hello—the house!'

The door swung open almost at once to his summons. A girl, perhaps twenty, tall, with dark eyes and an oval face capped with goldenrod hair, stepped out onto the porch. She looked at Ben questioningly.

'This the Melrose place?' he asked.

The girl nodded, half turned then as an elderly man followed closely by another woman, his wife, evidently, came through the doorway. The man squinted against the bright sunlight.

'I'm Whit Melrose. Something I can do for you?'

'Had a bit of trouble,' Kyle said, lifting his wounded arm slightly. 'Wondering if I could get some help.'

'He's been shot!' Mrs Melrose exclaimed, pushing forward.

Whit Melrose came off the porch hurriedly, head thrust forward. 'Don't I know you?'

'Ben Kyle—Henry Kyle was my pa. Knew you a few years back, before I left.'

Melrose bobbed his head. 'Sure! Thought you looked familiar,' he said, reaching up to steady Kyle as he dismounted. Over his shoulder, he added, 'Amy, you and Melinda get some water to heating ... And dig out that box of medicine.'

The women turned, disappeared into the house. Melrose, looping Ben's good arm about his neck, supported him to the kitchen where he jerked a straight-backed chair away from the table and eased Kyle onto it. Mrs Melrose was at the kitchen range pouring water from a kettle into a pan. The girl entered at the same moment, bringing a small wooden box containing cotton, bandages and several bottles of medicine.

Melrose ducked his head at her. 'My daughter, Melinda. Expect she was a little shaver when you pulled out.' He pointed to his wife. 'You probably remember Amy, my missus.'

Mrs Melrose looked over her shoulder and smiled. Melinda said, 'I remember you. You were over here a couple of times with your father.' She halted beside Ben. 'You'll have to

65

take off that shirt.'

Kyle was doing some remembering, too. It was hard to realize the attractive young woman standing so near him had once been a scrawny, freckled-face girl with yellow pigtails. The years had done marvelous things to her.

With Melrose's assistance, Ben removed the bloodied shirt, hung it over his knee. Melinda knelt, began to dab at the wound with a fold of cotton, pausing to dip the pad in the steaming water Amy Melrose placed on the floor beside her.

'Looks like a bullet hole,' the rancher said, sinking onto a chair. 'How'd it happen?'

'One of Park Halverson's bunch—'

The sharp intake of Amy Melrose's breath cut him short. He glanced to the older woman, saw worry mount into her eyes as she stepped back.

Whit Melrose leaned forward. 'What kind of trouble you got with him?'

'He's got a posse trailing me. Thinks I killed his son Bud.'

The rancher's jaw dropped. 'Bud—dead?'

Ben nodded. 'Had a run-in with him at Carmody's, so when they found him next morning the sheriff looked me up.' He paused, looked first at the rancher and then at the man's wife. 'Wasn't me. Had nothing to do with it. Just looked that way to Guyman, I guess.'

Melinda had not stopped during his

explanation. He winced when she applied some sort of disinfectant, leaned back wearily as she began to wrap a bandage around the wound.

Melrose, features stilled, rose, obtained a bottle of whiskey from a shelf, poured a generous drink into a water tumbler.

'Expect you need this,' he said. 'How long you been dodging Park?'

'Since early this morning,' Ben said, and downed the liquor.

'Then I reckon you'd better have a bite to eat, too,' the rancher said. 'Amy, fix him a plate.'

Mrs Melrose turned stiffly to the stove. Kyle glanced at Melinda, gathering her medical supplies. 'I'm obliged to you.'

She gave him a wide smile. 'It's only a flesh wound. Won't bother you much.' Rising, she reached for his shirt, 'I'll rinse this out.'

Kyle watched her cross the room, deposit the box on a shelf and then continue to an adjoining porch.

'Feeling better?'

Whit Melrose's question seized his attention. He grinned. 'The doctoring and that shot of whiskey make me feel like a new man. Glad I found you. Wasn't sure you'd still be here.'

The rancher rubbed his palms together. 'Won't say I haven't thought about pulling stakes. You know about your pa?'

'Know he's dead. If you're one of those who

67

helped bury him, I'm grateful. Whatever the cost was—'

Melrose shook his head. 'Forget that. Henry was my friend. Helped me plenty of times, same as he had some others. Who told you about him?'

'The sheriff.'

The rancher looked down. 'Yeah ... Should've figured it would be Walt.'

Ben frowned. 'He said it was just age. There more to it than that?'

Melrose settled back, watched Melinda enter, hang Kyle's shirt behind the stove. 'Well, no, not in the way you're maybe thinking. Henry was old, and I expect he was tired, like the rest of us. But Halverson was crowding him mighty hard—'

'Whit!' Amy Melrose broke in nervously.

'No harm in the truth, especially to Henry's own boy. Like I said, Park was going at him plenty strong, trying to make him sell out. Didn't ever hurt him, understand, just kept ragging him about it. Guess you could say your pa was hounded to death.'

Anger stirred through Ben Kyle. And then he shrugged. 'Should've never left the Warbucket—or else come home sooner. Could've maybe stopped it.'

The rancher's wife, her face set to disapproving lines, turned from the stove. Crossing the room, she set a plate heaped with sliced meat, warmed-over potatoes, beans, honey and biscuits on the table beside Ben. Melinda, bringing two cups and a pot of coffee, followed.

Amy Melrose drew back at once, halted at the window, began to stare out across the Flat. Melinda filled the cups, handed one to her father and, pushing the other at Kyle, sat down opposite him. Nodding to both, Ben took up his fork.

'Appreciate this,' he said, and glancing then to the rancher's wife, added, 'A fine meal, Mrs Melrose. Thank you.'

The older woman merely shrugged. Melrose flung her an impatient look, took a swallow of the coffee.

'You fixing to stay on?'

Ben paused in his eating, aware that Amy Melrose had turned, was watching him intently with worry-filled eyes. Across the table Melinda, too, showed interest but of a different kind.

'What I had in mind,' he said.

An audible sigh escaped the rancher's wife and her shoulders sagged. 'Now it'll get worse,' she murmured. Abruptly she wheeled. 'Why did you have to come back? Why couldn't you have stayed away?'

CHAPTER ELEVEN

Whit Melrose lunged to his feet, face red. 'Now, Amy—you've got no right—'

'I've got a right to expect a decent life—not one where I'm afraid every minute my husband's going to be killed, or my house burned down!'

'It won't be that way. We've had no trouble, not for quite a spell.'

'But it'll start all over again with him coming back ... Already has.'

Amy Melrose turned back to the window, began to sob quietly. Kyle rose, crossed to the stove and, taking his shirt off the peg where it had been hung by Melinda, pulled it on.

'I'm sorry,' he said. 'Didn't know my coming here would make it hard on you. Be getting my horse and moving on.'

'Not till you're finished eating,' the rancher said firmly; he grasped Ben's arm, forced him back to the table. 'Few more minutes ain't going to make no difference. Doubt that it matters, anyway. Where'll you go?'

Kyle's desire for food had vanished. Sipping at his cup of coffee, he shrugged. 'Got to find Bud's killer, clear my name.'

'Any idea who it was?'

'No. Was heading for Halverson's place when I caught that bullet. Aimed to talk to

Lonnie Rand. Where is Halverson's ranch?'

'The old Sanders spread—south of your range,' Melinda said.

Ben recalled the ranch, realized why Park Halverson wanted the Kyle property so badly. The two places adjoined; united they would form a sprawling piece of excellent cattle country.

'Who is Halverson? Don't recall the name.'

'Yon wouldn't,' Melrose replied. 'Moved in here about five years ago. Been busy growing ever since.'

'And doing it every way he can,' the girl said scornfully.

'Melinda!' Amy Melrose exclaimed, wheeling.

'I'm not afraid of Park Halverson, or any of his crowd!'

The rancher stared at his daughter, lifted a finger warningly. 'Nevertheless, you'll watch your tongue. I'm not running from trouble, but I won't ask for it, either.'

'Well, if I were a man—'

'You're not,' Melrose snapped, and swung his attention back to Ben. 'If you've got yourself crosswise with Park, you're in for a powerful lot of grief. He's big around here. Owns a lot of land, uses plenty that he don't. And folks, townspeople included, let him get by with just about anything.'

'Sort of got that idea,' Kyle said. 'That include the sheriff, too?'

'Walt Guyman's getting old, same as the rest of us. Ain't much fighting left in him.'

'And the deputy, Dane?'

'Reckon he's all right, only Walt's got his hands tied so's he can't do much.'

Kyle drained the last of his coffee. Melinda reached for the pot. He shook his head, got to his feet.

'Best I move on,' he said, glancing at Mrs Melrose. 'Wouldn't want that posse to see me around here.'

'Still going to Halverson's?'

'Only hope I've got. Lonnie was with Bud when it happened. He ought to know who jumped them.'

The rancher got up, frowning. 'If he does, funny he ain't told Park, instead of letting him think it was you.'

'Something that's been bothering me,' Ben admitted and turned toward the door. 'Want to thank you all again for your hospitality—and the doctoring,' he added, looking down at Melinda.

The girl smiled. 'If you're going to be hiding in the hills, you'll need food. I'll put some together,' she said and, rising, crossed to the cabinet beyond the stove, started filling a flour sack.

'You know Halverson's been using your range?' Melrose asked.

'Saw his stock when I rode in yesterday. Gave him till the end of the week to move the herd off.'

The rancher's jaw dropped again. 'You ordered Park to do that?'

'Sure—why not? It's my land.'

Melinda had paused, turned, was looking at him with a wide smile. Amy Melrose, however, spun, gave him a bitter, hopeless glance and hurried into another part of the house.

Whit shook his head slowly. 'Don't blame her too much, son. She's worried about what'll happen. Things sort of quieted down around here six, eight months ago. She's afraid now it'll all get started again.'

'My trouble,' Ben said. 'I'll keep it away from you.'

'It's everybody's trouble,' Melinda said quietly, moving up to him with the sack in her hand. 'Only nobody ever really stood up and did anything about it.'

'Easy to talk,' Melrose said wearily, thrusting out his hand. 'Good luck, and if I can do anything—'

Ben gripped the rancher's fingers, nodded his thanks to the rancher and his daughter, and moved to the door. Pushing open the screened panel, he stepped onto the porch, hesitated, his eyes on a line of riders far to the south. He hoped Amy Melrose was elsewhere in the house, had not noticed them.

'Anybody drops by looking for me, stretch the truth a bit, tell them you haven't seen me.'

Whit grinned. 'Not much for lying, but if it'll

73

help...'

'Be better for all of us,' Ben said and hurried to the waiting sorrel. Hanging the sack of grub on the saddle, he swung up, faced the rancher and his daughter. Melinda was smiling, her hand partly raised.

'Come back,' she called softly.

He nodded. 'I'll do that, once this is all settled,' he said and cut around the house toward the north, choosing the direction opposite to where he had noted the posse. He'd cause the Melroses no problems if he could help it.

CHAPTER TWELVE

Quickly placing the buildings of the ranch between himself and the distant riders, he veered to the west, effectively blocking all possible view. It was evident from Amy Melrose's reaction to his presence that she greatly feared the Diamond H owner. Whit, too, had been reserved in his offer to help; only Melinda had displayed defiance ... Quite a woman, that Melinda, he decided.

Gaining the slope he rode the sorrel into the brush, and once more altered course, now striking to the south. He was feeling much better as a result of the treatment accorded him at Melrose's, and his arm bothered him not at

74

all, fortunately being only a minor wound. It was the loss of blood coupled with an unnoticed hunger that had weakened him.

He saw the posse again a few minutes later when he topped out a low ridge. Halverson and his party were far to his left, working across a wide valley. At the moment they showed no indication of turning toward the Melrose place, but likely they would before the day was over.

Kyle rode on, convinced now more than ever that his key to salvation lay with Lonnie Rand. Only from him could he learn the identity of Bud's killer. Just how he could force the rider to talk—and before a witness—was something else. He'd manage it somehow.

The Sanders place ... He began to veer slightly east, taking as direct a route as possible. There was no time to waste; he must see and talk with Rand and be gone before Halverson returned with the posse. He would be cutting it thin as it was.

Park Halverson's dream was a fine one, he thought, staring out over the land—to combine thousands of acres of good grass amply supplied with permanent water.

Ben's thoughts halted on dead center. That was what lay behind Park Halverson's actions! The rancher, determined to have the Kyle property and so far unsuccessful, had seized an opportunity to make it possible. He was intentionally blaming the death of his son on

75

Ben as a means for removing him from the picture. The way would then be open for him to acquire the property through defaulted taxes.

It could be nothing else. Halverson knew Ben had not murdered Bud, was simply using the incident to gain his own ends. That the actual killer of his son was going unpunished apparently meant nothing to him.

Kyle swore grimly, pressed on. Having run up against Park Halverson twice, he could easily see how such was possible. The man, ruthless and tyrannical, thought only of himself and his desires, was ready and willing to sacrifice anything and anybody—even his own son apparently—to build his empire.

But the big redhead was due for a jolt, Ben vowed silently. He could bluster and threaten and rage all he wished, but he wasn't going to get away with it ... not this time. Lonnie Rand could be made to talk, and once he did the whole affair would be out in the open.

He glanced again toward the valley. The posse was no longer in sight. Slow worry mounted in Kyle. Had the rancher decided to turn back—or were the riders simply behind a ridge or within one of the numerous groves that dotted the Flat? He swore softly, blaming himself for not keeping closer watch. Likely he'd never get a better chance to talk with Lonnie Rand, but if Halverson was returning...

He would have to risk it. Urging the sorrel to

a faster lope, he rode on, passing his own property at a near half mile, noting as he did that Diamond H cattle still grazed on his range. Some time later he struck a vaguely familiar trail that led along the floor of a narrow dry wash for several miles, and then finally broke out onto a low butte that overlooked the Halverson ranch.

It was a barren, almost desolate place. Dedicated strictly to efficiency, it exhibited none of the niceties of a woman's touch—no flowers, no garden, few trees. It was simply an arrangement of buildings and a maze of corrals.

Smoke was rising from the metal stack of the kitchen but no one was in evidence. If he figured Halverson right, every hired hand except the cook and those riders necessary for the care of the herds were members of the posse. To the rancher bringing Ben down and exacting purported vengeance before a trial could be held would be foremost in mind.

Ben sat for a short time studying the main house and the crew's quarters, trying to decide in which he was most likely to find Rand. Being such a close companion of Bud, the odds were good he bunked with him and not the crew. He'd be smart to look there first, Ben decided, and keeping the brush and rocks in front of him as much as possible, he rode off the bluff.

He swung wide, approached the house from the opposite side where there were no other structures, and halted the sorrel in a clump of osage orange and tamarisk planted there by the previous owner as a windbreak. Securing the red to a stout sapling, he moved in toward the house, raking his memory for some recollection of the building's interior.

He had been inside only two or three times, and then he was small. But all the ranch houses were built more or less on the same plan: kitchen and dining room at one end, parlor at the other, with bedrooms in between.

The smoke from the kitchen indicated the presence of the cook at that point, so entry there was out of the question. The front door would be his best bet—assuming it had been left unlocked.

Moving quickly, he crossed the small, seldom used yard, stepped up onto the porch. Endeavoring to avoid squeaking boards, he made his way to the door, tried the knob. Disappointment slogged through him. It resisted solidly, appeared to have been nailed shut.

Kyle stepped back, threw his glance along the face of the building. Two windows broke the sameness of the long wall, both inaccessible because of shrubbery. He had no choice but to circle, attempt to enter the house from the side visible to the yard with its several structures and corrals.

That would be risky. He still believed that most of the Diamond H men would be with

Halverson, but there could be a hostler or two, yard hands, possibly even riders who had not been present when the party was organized, hanging around the place—and of course, the cook. But he'd come this far, and he had to see Rand.

Moving along the end of the house, Ben reached the corner, halted, spent several moments probing the yard and the smaller structures. No one appeared to be about, but that was no complete assurance; there could be a dozen men inside the bunkhouse, or the barn, and he'd have no way of knowing it.

Hair prickling along the back of his neck, he turned the corner, catfooted his way along the wall toward a door in the center of the building. Halfway there he went suddenly tense as the screen door to the kitchen swung open unexpectedly. Instantly he dropped low against the wall. An old man, stoop-shouldered, graying, wearing a once white but now heavily stained apron, entered the yard. Halting, he mopped at his lined face.

A moment later Lonnie Rand, lighting a cigarette, followed and took up a position beside the cook.

Surprise rippled through Ben Kyle. Rand was unmarked, bore no signs whatever of having been in a fight. Had he gone through what Park Halverson had claimed, he would have exhibited not only many bruises and scratches but undoubtedly would be wearing bandages as well.

Temper lifted within Kyle. Everything he had suspected of Halverson was coming true. He was being made a patsy of by the rancher—and he was wondering now if there actually had been a fight during which Bud was killed. In the next instant he realized there had to be truth in that; Bud Halverson was dead—unless everyone including Walt Guyman was lying.

But the answer to his own problems was standing before him, not ten strides away, and unarmed. That was all that mattered in that moment. Drawing his pistol, he stood upright.

'Lonnie—want to talk to you!'

Both Rand and the old cook whirled, taken completely by surprise. Lonnie, cigarette half raised to his lips, stared.

'You!'

'Right, me,' Kyle said quietly. 'I'm taking you into town. You're going to tell who killed Bud, get me off the hook—'

The steady drum of horses approaching the house from somewhere beyond the two men cut into Ben's words.

The posse ... Halverson had turned back, was likely coming in for a noon meal. Ben cursed his ill luck, gave the situation quick thought. Forcing Rand to accompany him was out of the question; there was no horse readily available for the man, and the sorrel, carrying double, would be unable to outrun the posse, which certainly would pursue immediately.

80

'I'll be coming for you again,' he said, backing toward the corner of the house. 'Don't get any ideas about leaving the country.'

Gaining the end of the structure, he wheeled, started for the sorrel at a hard run. Instantly Lonnie Rand's voice broke the hush.

'Park—he's here!'

The hammering of hooves became a loud thudding. Ben reached the windbreak, plunged into its dense screen. They would not be able to see him at first—the brush was too thick. He jerked the reins free, vaulted onto the saddle, aware that Halverson and the others, shouting back and forth, were streaming around the corner of the house.

Spurring the sorrel, he rode straight away, keeping the windbreak between himself and the building. With luck he should get a couple of hundred yards' start before one of them spotted him.

CHAPTER THIRTEEN

He made the hoped for distance, and then fortune forsook him. Abruptly he was on a low, bald hill with the nearest cover, a brush-filled arroyo running diagonally to his position, a good quarter mile away. But it was his only chance.

Veering the sorrel sharply, he roweled the

red deep, raced down the slope. Instantly yells broke out, drowned as quickly by two rapid gunshots. Kyle bent low over the saddle, threw his glance toward the windbreak. Halverson, followed by the remainder of the posse, was breaking clear of the tamarisk, coming on fast.

More guns began to blast. Dust spurted up around the sorrel. At such distance Ben knew he offered no good target, but the big red horse was something else. If they contrated on him ... He hunched lower, called on the sorrel for more speed and began taking advantage of every obstacle, each dip and high place encountered. He looked ahead anxiously. They were almost to the arroyo.

Suddenly they were at its steep bank, plunging down. The sorrel, lathered and sucking for wind, slowed as the tough undergrowth hindered his way, then gathered his strength, rushed on. The shouting stopped, as well as the shooting, but not for long, Ben knew. It was simply that he was no longer a visible target.

Halverson and the others would be on his heels again shortly. Raising himself, he tried to see beyond the tips of the brush. The wash seemed to run on indefinitely, possibly clear to the Warbucket, but there was no guarantee. Besides, progress was slow and he could not hope to make passage with little noise. Best he climb out of the gash, find—

Ben heard the posse again at that moment:

the hard clatter of their arrival at the edge of the arroyo, Halverson yelling to spread out, work the brush. Then came the rattling and popping as the riders rode down into the wash, began forcing their way through the undergrowth.

The arroyo spread wider and its banks became lower as larger trees began to appear. He was coming to more open country, Kyle saw, and would soon run out of cover.

He glanced about. The dark point of a grove loomed up to his right, and faintly visible through the scatter of trees, he saw the red clay face of a butte. Hope lifted within him; he was nearing the brakes—hadn't realized he was anywhere near that area.

Without hesitation he swerved the laboring sorrel from the sandy floor of the wash, bucking brush, wincing as thin branches slashed his face and arms with stinging force, finally reached the bank. Again he swung down grade, taking advantage of a bulging shoulder of sand and rock in hopes it would further screen him from the posse, and then on firmer ground, spurred for the trees.

Gaining their protection, he whipped into a thicket of wild gooseberries, dropped instantly from the saddle to lower his silhouette, and turned his attention to the arroyo.

In only moments he saw the first rider, Dave Zuda. Pistol drawn, the gunman was walking his horse at a fast beat, head thrust forward, eyes scanning the brush. Behind him came Tom Dane, and almost abreast the deputy were Halverson and Walt Guyman. The balance of the party was scattered beyond and behind them, forming a line that stretched entirely across the arroyo.

Ben grinned tightly, watching them press on past the shoulder where he had turned off, and continue on down slope. He had given them the slip—for a while. Soon it would become apparent he was not ahead of them; they would halt, double back. Eventually someone would pick up the sorrel's prints.

Grim, he looked toward the bluff. He could see very little of it, had no idea of how extensive the formation might be. But again it was his solitary choice. Turning to the red, he stepped into the saddle, put the horse to a slow lope through the aisles between the trees.

Reaching the butte, he pulled up short. It was much larger than he had expected, extending for a good half mile to the south. Flowing out from its base was a broad bowl-like depression well filled with scrub junipers, cedars, rabbit-brush and other ragged growth.

Movement a short distance away caught his attention. He watched intently, saw the friction-pointed tips of a steer's horns break through the undergrowth, followed by a lean, tan and white shape ... an old maverick living out his life in the brakes. Likely there were many more of his kind nearby.

The old steer offered a solution. Moving fast, Ben rode down the sandy slope into the brush, making certain to leave a definite trail. Once well in the undergrowth, he cut right, fought his way back to the foot of the butte. Then dismounting, and leaving the red well hidden, he climbed to a lower ledge on the face of the bluff and there, shielded by a rocky ridge and an irregular hedge of snakeweed, sprawled out to await the arrival of the posse.

Park Halverson, face glowing with anger, appeared first at the rim of the bowl. Pulling to a halt he stared at the wild maze of tangled growth. A moment later Zuda and Dane were beside him. Finally Guyman and the others broke into view.

'Lost him, Goddammit!' the rancher shouted. He wheeled to the sheriff. 'Wouldn't be happening if you'd been on the job, looking after things the way you ought.'

'Had him locked up tight,' Guyman said, shrugging.

Halverson removed his hat, mopped at his features with a forearm. 'You ain't cutting it no more, Walt. Might as well admit it—'

'Something moving down there!' Tom Dane said, pointing.

The rancher stood in his stirrups, gazed at the brush. After a bit he settled back. 'Damned stray. Place is full of them.'

'Could spread out, make a drive through there,' the deputy suggested.

'Ain't enough men for that, and dark's coming on. Couldn't tell if something moving was him or one of them damned strays.'

'Good fifteen miles to the other side,' a rider commented. 'And I'm getting hungry.'

Two or three other voices echoed the thought. Halverson, clearly ignoring Guyman, turned to Dane. 'Well, we ain't giving him up. Deputy, where you figure he'll come out?'

'Only a couple of places where he can,' Dane said readily. 'Sides are pretty steep—'

'Might double back,' Zuda said. 'He's smart—smart enough to figure we'll be watching—'

'He ain't smart enough!' Halverson snarled. 'We'll leave two men here. You, Deputy, take a couple more and get around on the other side—'

'Going to have to eat,' one of the members said, 'and this horse of mine's about done in.'

'Coming to that. Rest of us'll go back to my place, get us a bite of grub and swap horses. Then we'll swing back, relieve them that's been doing the watching.'

'Ought to work fine,' Tom Dane said, spurring his mount around. 'Who's coming with me?'

Halverson made an indefinite motion with his thick hand. 'Oh, take Culver and Pete Morris ... Kansas, you and Romero stay here.'

The rider directly behind Zuda bobbed his head, scrubbed at his jaw. 'Sure thing, boss,

86

but don't be too long sending that relief. I'm getting mighty lean.'

'Won't be more'n a couple of hours,' the rancher said, kneeing his horse about. He paused, pointed to a high spot a hundred yards farther down. 'Set yourself up there. Expect you can pretty much see the whole place from them rocks. You get a look at him heading for the other side, fire a shot so's the deputy and the others will know to get ready.'

The riders began to wheel around, their horses shouldering one another in the small clearing. Walt Guyman and Halverson at the front were now forced to wait, allow the others to move out. The old lawman, resting his weight on one leg, studied the rancher.

'I ain't appreciating your looking to that deputy of mine for everything,' he said coldly. 'Happens I'm the sheriff, not him.'

'I deal with the man who can do the job,' Halverson snapped.

'Meaning I can't?'

'The hat fits, put it on,' the rancher said.

'Day comes when I figure it will, I'll do just that. Right now there's something I'd like you to be explaining.'

Halverson turned on his saddle, glared at the lawman. 'Explaining's something I figure I don't have to do, but what's bothering you?'

'Lonnie. Got a good look at him back there. He ain't been in no fight—not the way you claimed.'

The rancher shrugged. 'Didn't do much fighting. Kyle clubbed him over the head with his gun, I reckon. Knocked him cold first off.'

Guyman considered that, settled back on his saddle as the way before him cleared and his horse began to move out. 'Still, seems he ought to show something.'

Whatever reply Park Halverson made to the lawman was unheard by Ben Kyle.

CHAPTER FOURTEEN

Kyle lay on the ledge, listened to the sounds of the departing posse. Walt Guyman was having thoughts about Rand, too, and the need to get with Lonnie, force him to talk, was becoming more important. But such would be a considerable chore; Halverson, obviously, was keeping the rider under wraps, permitting him to speak with no outsider.

Why?

The rancher's excuse had been that Lonnie was badly beaten in the fracas that brought about the death of his son ... yet Rand showed no effects. There was some deeper, more pertinent reason for Halverson's actions, one that related directly to him; and he'd never clear himself of the murder charge until he brought that reason to the surface.

Delaying until the men ordered by the

rancher to remain had taken their place below on the designated point, Kyle crawled from the ledge and made his way to where he had hidden the sorrel. He had little fear of being seen or heard by the riders as long as he employed ordinary care, since they were some distance away.

But he took no chances. Freeing the red, he led the horse out of the brush and up onto the flat overlooking the tangled swale. Once well into the grove he mounted, swung south, going away from both Halverson's ranch and the opposite side of the brake where Tom Dane and the men siding him would be establishing a watch.

His problem now was Lonnie Rand. But how could he get to the rider, compel him to talk? Returning to the Diamond H was out of the question, and if Halverson confined him there, kept him virtually a prisoner...

Guyman or Tom Dane. There was the answer. As lawmen they would have the authority to bring the man in for questioning, assuming Ben could convince them that Rand, intimidated by Park Halverson, was not telling the truth.

Which one could he trust? Guyman, apparently, suspected all was not as the rancher claimed where Lonnie was concerned, but would he have the courage to buck Halverson? That he was fighting to hold his badge was evident—and the rancher was a powerful man with wide influence.

Tom Dane? Possibly he was the better bet. The deputy's soaring ambition would encourage him to undertake anything that would tend to further undermine Guyman's position, put himself in a stronger light. But that same ambition could work the other way; currying favor, he might take the matter to Halverson and thereby strengthen his relationship with the rancher.

Ben shrugged wearily; boiling it down, he doubted if Guyman had the guts and he feared Tom Dane would take advantage of the opportunity to enhance his own cause. It was like being caught between a rock and a hard place, but he could see no other means for forcing the truth from Rand.

There was no one else he could turn to. The townspeople would venture nothing that would endanger their status with Halverson; and Whit Melrose would reflect the attitude of other ranchers on the Flat—sympathetic, agreeable, but unwilling to act.

He had no choice but to depend on the lawmen—one or the other; as near as he could figure it didn't really matter which one. The odds were about equal insofar as the possibility of failure was concerned.

That decision presented further problems— how to get in touch with Guyman or Dane. Common sense dictated the necessity for meeting with them alone, and at the moment both were in the company of either Halverson or his men.

Oak Springs ...

Sooner or later one or the other, perhaps even both, would return to the settlement. The need for checking on the office and seeing that all was well in the town would be apparent. If he were waiting nearby, force whichever lawman it happened to be to listen, using a gun if need be, he'd at least make a few facts known and possibly get something started.

It seemed the only answer. Halting, Ben Kyle glanced around, got his bearings. He had been moving steadily southwest, skirting the foot of a long grass-carpeted ridge. Immediately he swung the sorrel east.

He should reach Oak Springs around dark, he figured, making allowances for a circuitous route that would enable him to travel most of the distance through periodic groves and stands of brush.

There was still some light when he rode into the tall willows growing along the bank of the Warbucket and dismounted. There he stalled out an hour, eating a cold meal from the provisions Melinda Melrose had placed in the flour sack. When it was totally dark, he went to the saddle, rode on toward town on a well-beaten path along the edge of the river.

There was a vacant building, he recalled, across the street from Carmody's. While it was several doors below and on the opposite side from the jail, it would afford an ideal point from which to observe the lawmen's quarters. He should be able to reach it with ease, approaching as he was from the rear.

Coming to the line of buildings, he again halted, drawing the sorrel in behind a small shed standing at the back of the first structure.

Carmody's was already going strong, and the sounds of voices and music reached him clearly. He could see little of the street where he sat but there would be several persons abroad, soaking in the evening's coolness as they window-shopped along the sidewalk.

Urging the sorrel on, he singled out the empty building, angled quickly toward its gloomy, squat shape. There was no nearby shelter for the red, and he saw it would be necessary to leave the horse in the open unless the rear door was large enough to admit him.

Reaching the structure, he dismounted, moved up to the wall. There was no door at all, he discovered, only a gaping doorway, and being of usual size, much too small for the sorrel's bulk.

He glanced up and down the row of buildings. The hotel's stable was a hundred yards distant—much too far for safety if it became necessary to depart in a hurry. No other barns or sheds were available; as he had feared, he'd have to leave the big red standing in the alley.

Drawing the horse in as close to the wall as

possible, he snubbed him tight and entered the building. Once it had been a store of some sort, there being a small room across the rear, a much larger area fronted by large, now broken windows, on the street side. Shelves lined the walls, and a crude counter extended almost the full width of the room.

Dragging up an empty nail keg, Ben sat down behind the counter. From there he had a view of the jail to his right, Carmody's on the left, and a generous portion of the street in between.

The broken windows admitted outside sounds and the rough counter protected him from the eyes of passersby who might glance in as they strolled along the sidewalk. Taken on the whole he could not be in a much better location—except for the sorrel. Anyone walking down the alley, or crossing at some nearby point to reach the street, would notice the big red, and that possibility set up a deep worry within him.

But perhaps he wouldn't have to wait long.

CHAPTER FIFTEEN

Time wore on.

A stagecoach arrived, slid to a stop in front of the hotel, disgorged its cargo of worn, dust-covered passengers. A man in a buggy raced

93

down the street, halted before a house bearing the sign: DR. AMOS JAHN. Leaping from the vehicle, he rushed into the vine-covered cottage. Moments later he reappeared with a second man, who was carrying a small satchel and pulling on his coat. Both climbed hastily into the buggy, sped back up the street.

Gradually traffic along the walks dwindled. Lamps went out but business at Carmody's remained brisk, the racket arising there overriding the faint tones of choir practice at the Baptist church. Finally that, too, ceased, as if in defeat, and there was only Carmody's and a solitary dog barking forlornly at the star-studded sky.

From that point on it was only a matter of checking out riders entering the street. Ben missed no one, saw all who came into town—usually headed for Carmody's—and not one was either Walt Guyman or Deputy Dane.

Near dawn the town physician, Jahn, returned, and then an hour or so later, as Ben's worry over the sorrel standing in the alley increased with the approach of daylight, two men, slumped on their saddles, entered the street. He recognized them at once as the pair Halverson had stationed near the ledge at the brake where he had hidden. Evidently the rancher had kept them there throughout the night.

The two separated, each going home, he supposed, and he began to wonder if the posse was disbanding. It didn't seem likely; chances were they simply had returned to rest, get a bit of sleep while others of the party continued the search. If so, then Dane and the men with him should be riding in also, assuming they didn't elect to do their sleeping at Halverson's ranch.

Kyle stirred impatiently ... There was always an *if* to reckon with, to make firm plans impossible. He rose, walked to the rear of the building, glanced up and down the alley. No one was around as yet, but eventually men would be up and about, doing their chores, heading for jobs—and the sorrel would be noticed, curiosity would be aroused.

He wished now he had thought to leave the red at Carmody's hitchrack. No one would have taken note of him there, simply believe him to be waiting for an owner inside enjoying himself. But it was too late to think about that. Restless, he returned to the nail keg, sat down.

Shortly before eight o'clock his patience was rewarded. There was a sudden thud of hoofbeats, and then Tom Dane, accompanied by two riders, wheeled into the settlement. All went directly to Carmody's, then returned to the street, split and went their separate ways.

Kyle watched the deputy climb back onto his horse, approach, pass by and halt at Doc Jahn's office. He remained there for several minutes and then, reappearing, crossed over and entered the sheriff's office.

Immediately Ben hurried to the sorrel.

Mounting, he swung back to the path near the river, skirted Carmody's and, unnoticed by anyone, rode to the rear of the jail. The back door would be unlocked, he recalled, thanks to the deputy.

Drawing his pistol, he tried the knob. The panel opened and he slipped inside quietly. Moving slow, he traveled the short hallway, stopped when he reached the corner of the cell. Through the lattice of bars he could see Dane sitting at Guyman's desk, digging about in a lower drawer for something. Gun leveled, Kyle stepped into the center of the room.

Dane glanced up, startled. Shock spread across his dark face.

'What the hell ...?'

'Just sit quiet, Deputy,' Ben cut in, kicking the front door shut and sliding the bolt. 'All I'm here for is conversation.'

Tom Dane's features hardened. 'You been waiting for me all night?' he asked, looking closely at Ben.

'All night,' Kyle answered, moving in nearer.

A hard grin shaped the deputy's mouth. 'And Halverson with half the county out beating the hills—'

'Seems he's running the whole show,' Kyle observed scornfully. 'Make a man wonder who the law really is.'

'I'm wearing the badge.'

'And Guyman?'

96

'Still the sheriff—'

'But not for long if you've got anything to say about it . . . Keep your hands on top of that desk where I can see them, Deputy.'

Dane shrugged, leaned forward, placed his palms flat on the dusty surface. He moved his head slightly. 'I'll say this, you've got one hell of a lot of guts coming right into town like this. What're you after?'

'You or Guyman. Didn't make much difference which.'

The deputy's eyes narrowed. 'What for?'

'Want you to do some listening. Everybody's so damned trigger-happy a man can't get a word said.'

'Anything you've got to say won't do you much good,' Dane said dryly. 'Not now, anyway.'

'Should—if that badge you're wearing counts for much. Thing I want you to get straight is that I never killed Bud Halverson.'

The deputy smiled. 'Expected you'd say that. Every man I've arrested claimed he was innocent.'

'Here's one that is. Now, I don't know what's going on around here but there's one thing sure, I'm not standing pat for Halverson or anybody else making me their goat.'

'So?'

'I want Lonnie Rand brought in so's I can talk to him. Claims to have been with Bud when he was murdered, got beat up himself.

He's lying. Saw him yesterday and there wasn't a scratch on him. He'd been in no fight like Halverson said. They're covering up something—both of them.'

Tom Dane stared intently at Kyle, a deep frown on his face.

'Stands to reason Lonnie knows who the killer is, and I aim to get it out of him. No chance long as Halverson keeps him cooped up on his ranch. Almost got a skin full of lead yesterday trying.'

Dane continued to stare, seemingly at a loss.

Ben leaned forward. 'Idea is to arrest Lonnie for something—anything—get him in here so's we can fire a few questions at him without Halverson being around. I figure he'll start spouting quick. Looks like the kind who can't stand the heat.

'Once he starts talking we'll have the answer. We'll know who killed Bud and I'll be in the clear ... And for you—well, it's plain you're after Guyman's job. I don't give a hang who wears the star around this town, but it'll be a feather in your hat to nail down the real killer.'

Dane wagged his head slowly. 'You're either the smartest or the dumbest—'

'Look at it any way you like. Only thing I'm out for is to prove I'm not guilty of killing Bud Halverson. Sure, I had trouble with him, not once but twice. I didn't like him, but I didn't hate him either. Expect I felt sorry for him more than anything else.

'His pa's something different. He's a man who makes it easy to hate him and I wouldn't spit in his face if he was dying of thirst. Expect Bud would be alive today if it wasn't for him and his high-handed way of doing things. Running rough-shod over somebody got his son killed for him.'

Ben paused, studied Dane, wondered if he were getting anywhere with the lawman. The deputy's face betrayed nothing, only a strange sort of patience.

'All I can say is Park Halverson deserves what he got, but the boy didn't ... Not here or there, however. It's me I'm thinking about. I want this deal straightened out so's I can settle down on my ranch, start doing the things I've got in mind. Lonnie Rand's the key. You willing to work with me, bring him in so's we can get to the truth?'

Tom Dane settled back, eyes fixed on Kyle's intent face.

'Like I said, either you're smart or you're dumber than hell. I ain't bringing Lonnie in for a talk. Nobody is. We found him dead early this morning.'

CHAPTER SIXTEEN

Ben Kyle recoiled as if he had been struck, but his eyes never left those of the deputy. Pistol still leveled, he moved to the side, sat down on one of the chairs placed along the wall.

'Ought to back my story,' he said slowly. 'Whoever killed Bud got to him—'

'You,' Dane said flatly. 'That's what everybody's thinking.'

Kyle sighed. 'Expect they would.'

'Plain to them. Lonnie was the only witness. What he'd tell the judge would put a rope around the killer's neck. Was his death warrant ... you had to kill him so's he couldn't testify.'

'Only I didn't,' Ben said wearily. He shook his head. 'Rand was my only chance.'

He could forget Lonnie Rand. That road was now closed to him; there was nothing else to do but keep digging, find another way to prove his innocence.

'When was Lonnie killed?'

'Sometime last night. Found him this morning.'

'Where?'

'Halverson's barn.'

Ben frowned. 'You there?'

'Yeah, me and most of the posse. We'd been relieved after standing watch for you at that damned brake. Was just sitting down to breakfast at Halverson's when one of the hands came busting in and said Lonnie was lying dead out there.

'We all went down to have a look. Wasn't a pretty sight. Beat up bad, just like Bud. Another reason everybody figures it was the

100

same killer.'

'Me.'

Dane nodded. 'You. Only natural to look at it that way.'

Kyle swore angrily. 'Jumping at things, that's what you're doing. Making up your minds fast. Seems you and the sheriff and everybody else around is real good at that. Makes no difference that you might be cracking down on the wrong man.'

'Evidence—that's about all we can go on—'

'Evidence! You don't have any. Halverson says it's so, and you take that as evidence.'

'Maybe I should have said motive ... You and Bud had trouble, a fight. You didn't like him or his pa. There's your reason. Now maybe you didn't intend to kill him, just teach him a lesson, but you sort of got carried away, lost your head.'

'And then because Lonnie Rand was killed in the same way, I'm given credit for his murder, too. All adds up fine except for one thing: you're wrong from the very start.'

Tom Dane only shrugged, glanced toward the window. Immediately Kyle rose. Apparently the deputy was expecting a visitor, probably the men who had ridden in with him, prepared now to rejoin the posse.

'Where you meeting Halverson and the others?'

The deputy showed momentary surprise. Then, 'Me and some of the others figure to work the country south of the brake. Others plan to spread out, cover the Flat and hills. Won't be no place safe for you.'

Kyle's laugh was harsh. 'From that I figure you look at it same as the others—that I'm guilty.'

'Not sure of it one way or another. Seems that way, but fact is I'm interested in finding the man who done it and bringing him in for trial ... you or whoever.'

'Sounds good,' Ben said dryly, 'but you know damn well you're blowing in the breeze. Halverson'll never let you do it.'

'Halverson wouldn't have anything to say about it if I got my hands on the man first! Be easier if you gave yourself up now.'

Ben studied the deputy narrowly for a few moments, finally shook his head. 'Maybe you'd try. Haven't got you exactly square in my mind yet, but I can't afford to take the chance. Where'd you say you were to meet?'

'Rocky Point,' Dane answered, and caught at his words abruptly. He colored slightly, grinned. 'At noon. Why? You plan to be there?'

'Never can tell,' Ben said. 'Stand up.'

Dane rose to his feet, hands lifted. Kyle stepped in close, lifted the deputy's six-gun from its holster, thrust it under his belt.

'If you're smart as I think you are,' he said, backing toward the hallway, 'you'll stay put for five minutes after I've closed the door.

Could lock you up but you did me a favor, so now I'll do you one by not putting you in your own cell.'

Dane nodded, pointed at his weapon. 'My gun...'

'It'll be outside, empty. Don't want you taking potshots at me while I'm riding off.'

The deputy shrugged, motioned at the cabinet on the wall containing several rifles and shotguns, all under chain and padlock.

'Do better with one of those, was I of a mind to try.'

'Expect you could at that,' Ben said, returning and picking up the ring of keys on the desk. 'Find these with your iron.'

Again he paused. 'One thing's still bothering me—that favor of yours. You fix it so's I could escape to make the sheriff look bad, or were you planning to cut me down when I stepped through the back door to make yourself look good?'

Tom Dane smiled. 'Reckon that's something you'll never know the answer to, mister,' he drawled.

'Maybe I already do,' Kyle said and backed the rest of the corridor's length. 'Be seeing you,' he added, and stepped quickly into the open.

Tossing Dane's pistol and the keys a dozen yards farther down, he wheeled to the sorrel, mounted and struck for the hills at a fast gallop. He didn't think the deputy would be foolish enough to take any chances but he couldn't be certain of it.

Reaching the first flare of timber, he slowed the red, glanced back. A roll of land hid all but the roofs of the tallest buildings and he had no way of knowing if Dane had followed him into the alley. It didn't matter. He was in the clear.

In the clear.

The phrase echoed bitterly in his mind. Clear of the settlement perhaps, but worse off than ever. Before the sun was at high noon the hills and flats would be crawling with men all seeking his blood for not one but two murders—and his one hope of proving himself innocent was gone.

He rode on, pointing for the higher hills to the south and west ... Give it up ... Forget the whole thing ... Get the hell out of the Warbucket country while still alive ... There's nothing left.

But running would not bring an end to it, There'd be no place he could go. Every lawman, every bounty hunter out to make a dollar, every over-zealous citizen from one end of the country to the other would be on the watch for him, hoping to bring him down.

No, better to settle it now or else forget, forever, all hope of peace and normal existence. But how does a man prove himself innocent of crime when he has nothing to go on—no witnesses, no alibis, not even a friend?

Suddenly Ben Kyle drew up straight on the

saddle, a glimmer of thought pegging persistently at his brain. It was something Tom Dane had said about the way Lonnie Rand had died, how they had found him.

It wasn't much and he couldn't exactly put his finger on it, but a pattern was taking shape, loose strings were pulling in, disappearing. He grinned tightly ... Thin, but at least a beginning. He looked back over his shoulder. No one was on his trail. Immediately he cut right, started for the Halverson ranch.

CHAPTER SEVENTEEN

The morning was warm, pleasant. Ben Kyle thought of the ranch he could build, the fine life he could live once the threat to him was gone. And Melinda Melrose. He had realized more and more during the continuing press of events how very much she was figuring in his future. He *had* to clear things up—so much depended upon it.

The answer lay at Halverson's. He wasn't certain just what it was or how he would go about finding it, but a voice within him insisted his proof was there. Something didn't jibe, didn't add up. If he could pin it down, drag it into the open...

Motion in the deep brush to his right sent alarm racing through him. His hand dropped swiftly to the pistol at his side as he brought the sorrel to quick halt.

'Don't reach for that hogleg, mister,' a voice coming from the opposite warned coldly. 'Not unless you're aching to get a hole blowed through your middle. Raise 'em!'

Cursing his own carelessness, Ben lifted his arms slowly. He knew the country was working with Halverson men and posse members recruited from town; he should have known better than ride blindly along, his mind on everything but the possibility of danger.

A squat, beefy rider with a full, black moustache came from the shadows of the undergrowth to one side. From a point directly opposite a younger, smooth-faced puncher appeared. Ben swore again. They had been waiting for him, had evidently spotted him from the distance and, separating, had set up an ambush on either side of the trail. Obligingly, he had ridden straight into their trap.

'You been making yourself mighty scarce around here,' the older man said, squinting at Kyle. 'Get his gun, Ollie.'

The second rider eased in from the rear, lifted Kyle's pistol from its holster. 'What'll we do with him?'

'Take him to the ranch, then go get the boss. Them was his orders. Got something we can tie him up with?'

Ollie briefly probed through his pockets,

shook his head. 'He'll be all right till we reach the ranch, then we can salt him down.'

The older man nodded. 'Just keep your iron on him. He tries running, we'll both cut loose on him. Don't reckon it makes much difference to Park what shape he's in, long as we got him. Move out, mister.'

Kyle lowered his hands carefully, touched the sorrel with his spurs. As the red started on, he glanced at his captors. They rode one on either side and slightly to the rear, pistols leveled at his back. Escape at the moment would be an impossibility, if he wanted to remain alive.

Best he bide his time. The pair might get careless, or possibly it would be better to wait until they had reached the ranch. A better opportunity might present itself there. He grinned bleakly; he had wanted to visit Halverson's but not exactly under these conditions.

An hour later they rode into the swale where the ranch buildings and the collection of corrals clustered. Skirting the windbreak, they pulled to a stop at the hitchrack a short distance from the kitchen door. The cook appeared at once, stepping out onto the small, square landing. He stared and then his wrinkled, red face pulled into a grin.

'Well now, Clete! Looks like you and Ollie've gone and caught yourself a mighty big fish.'

'For a fact, Rufe,' the beefy man said laconically.

'Where'd you nab him?'

'Down near the spring,' Clete said, not taking his eyes off Ben as he dismounted. 'Was working a hunch. Everybody's off, scattered from hell to breakfast. Figured was I him they was looking for, I'd pick me a spot in the middle and just take it easy, let them do all the running. Was what he was doing.'

Ollie had swung from his mount, too, stepped to the sorrel's head. 'Climb down, and don't try nothing.'

Kyle eased from the saddle, stood silent awaiting further instructions.

'Bring him inside,' the cook said. 'Be easier watching. One of you'd better go fetch Halverson.'

'Aim to do that soon's we truss him up. You got some coffee made?'

'Always got coffee made,' Rufe answered, turning to the door. 'You better find the boss, howsomever.'

Clete grunted. 'Another five minutes ain't going to make no difference,' he said, prodding Ben with his pistol. 'Get in there, killer.'

Nerves taut and watching narrowly, Ben trailed the old cook into the kitchen, closely followed by Clete and Ollie. The room was hot and a large kettle on the stove was burbling noisily, emitting the appetizing odor of stewing vegetables and beef.

'Where'll we put him?' Ollie asked.

'Tie him down in one of them chairs,' Clete said. 'Get some rope.'

Ollie holstered his weapon, wheeled, started for the door. In that instant Ben Kyle recognized opportunity. His jaw clamped shut. Either he'd make it or he'd die, 'cause to allow himself to be bound and rendered helpless until Park Halverson arrived was death for certain.

He spun, the motion only a blur. Catching the old cook by the arm, he flung him straight into Clete. The squat rider yelled, went crashing back against a table, tangled in Rufe's threshing legs and arms.

At the first sound Ollie had wheeled. Before he could draw his weapon Kyle was on him, slashing him across the eyes with the back of a hand, driving his knee into the young puncher's belly.

Ollie gasped, buckled forward. Ben drove a stiff right to his jaw, spun him half around, and pivoted to meet Clete, scrambling to regain his footing.

Kyle reached out, caught the man by his shirt front, dragged him to his knees. From the tail of an eye he saw Rufe rushing in, a meat cleaver raised above his head.

Ben slammed Clete back against the shattered table, dodged as the cook swung his vicious weapon. Off balance, Rufe stumbled by. Ben smashed a fist into the older man's jaw, dropped him solidly to the floor.

109

Leaping over Rufe's stiffening body, Ben closed with Ollie, on his feet and reaching for the pistol still in his holster. The weapon came up, met Kyle's arcing foot. It flew from the puncher's grasp, sailed across the room.

'Goddamn you—you—'

The enraged voice of Clete warned Ben that the husky rider was moving in again. Seizing Ollie by the wrist, he whipped him around, sent him crashing into the older man. For the second time Clete was driven back against the table and into the jumble of splintered wood.

Soaring anger and frustration at last breaking through and having its violent way with him, Ben Kyle lunged at the sprawling men. Grasping Ollie by the arm, he jerked the rider to a sitting position, put everything he had into a right to the man's jaw. Ollie groaned, wilted. Two down.

A gun blast suddenly rocked the heat-filled room. Glass shattered as a bullet smashed a window. Ben hurled himself at Clete, clawed for the pistol in the man's hand. His fingers closed in a tight grip around Clete's wrist. Mouthing curses the Halverson man fought to dislodge Kyle's weight.

Ben struck him sharply across the nose, hung tight to the hand grasping the pistol. Heaving mightily, Clete managed to get free of Kyle's hindering body, drew away an arm's length.

He lashed out with his booted foot, caught

110

Ben a stunning blow in the ribs, sent a surge of pain racing through Kyle's body.

Ben lunged then, brought his knotted fist across in a sledging drive, caught the puncher flush on the chin. Clete groaned as his head thumped against the floor. His body went slack.

Sucking for wind Ben snatched up the pistol, staggered to his feet. Crossing the room he recovered his own weapon, Clete's and Ollie's. Holstering his, he tossed the others into the wood box beside the stove.

Fury was still driving him relentlessly, and ignoring his body's crying need to pause, rest, he snatched a stained rag from a nail in the wall, ripped it down the center and rolled each into improvised rope. Straddling Ollie, he turned the rider onto his belly, bound his wrists together tightly.

He then followed a like procedure with Clete, and finished, dragged both men past the cook, sitting up, rubbing dazedly at his jaw, and piled both in a corner.

Spinning, he picked up the cleaver, faced Rufe. 'You're next!' he rasped hoarsely.

The old cook drew back, his watery eyes flooded with fear. 'Not me!' he yelled. 'I ain't wanting none of this!'

'You've got it anyway!' Kyle snarled, his body heaving. 'One way out—start talking!'

CHAPTER EIGHTEEN

'I don't know nothing!' the cook cried, squirming anxiously. 'That's the gospel truth!'

'Maybe you do, and maybe you don't. But you're going to talk, tell me everything I want to know. Else—' Kyle paused, raised the cleaver, buried its point a half inch in the wall.

'Just you keep remembering,' he said then, calmly freeing the blade, 'they can't hang me but one time. Understand?'

The old man bobbed his head frantically.

'Lonnie was my one chance,' he said in a low voice. 'Whoever killed him knew that. He ever say anything to you?'

'No, sir, nothing.'

'Who talked to him after I was here yesterday?'

'Nobody much. Park and them others went chasing after you, was gone quite a spell. Later most of them come back.'

'Lonnie still here?'

'Sure. Park told him to stay in the house. Said he didn't want him traipsing around none.'

'Who talked to him then?'

'Oh, reckon Park and Dave Zuda. Couple other boys. Didn't pay much mind. Remember the sheriff asking him how he felt.'

'What did Lonnie say?'

The cook shrugged nervously. 'Said he was doing fine, and getting mighty sick of just setting around.'

'How long had Halverson been keeping him penned up?'

'Since the morning they found Bud.'

Ben considered what he had heard so far, could find nothing of value. Brushing away the sweat on his face, he said, 'You here when Lonnie and Halverson came from town the morning Bud was found?'

'Reckon so. Always here.'

'Lonnie look like he'd been in a fight?'

'Was a bit mussed up, clothes, I mean. Said he'd got a right smart rap on the head.'

'Wearing a bandage?'

'Nope. Didn't see one.'

Kyle shook his head. 'Lonnie was lying. I don't think he was in a fight. I figure he ducked out, kept out of the way while someone worked Bud over.'

Rufe grunted. 'Sounds like Lonnie, sure enough. Not long on much except bellyaching and talking. Always done a lot of whining. That's why Park told him to go on last night when he was beefing so loud about being cooped up.'

Ben Kyle's attention drew to a sharp point. 'Told him to do what?'

'Go to town. Was bitching so about it Park finally up and told him to saddle and get going. Said if he wanted to chance getting his head

113

blowed off—by you—it was his funeral.'

'And Lonnie took him up on it?'

'Not right away. Reckon what Park said about you sort of cooled him down some. But later on he went.'

Ben leaned forward slightly. 'You actually see him go?'

'Said I did!' the old man replied testily, mopping at his face with a corner of his apron.

Kyle fingered the cleaver. 'Tell me about it.'

Rufe wagged his head helplessly. 'Was later, like I said. Everybody was setting around, resting, drinking coffee and talking. They was fixing to hit the saddle again and go looking for you. Park said—'

'The hell with that! What about Lonnie?'

Rufe gulped, continued hastily. 'Recollect seeing him come into the room wearing his gun. Told Park he wouldn't be gone long, just wanted some saloon drinking, and maybe to spark the girls a bit. Then him and Park went out into the yard.

'Dave Zuda was setting out there on the bench and he got up. Last I seen the three of them was just sort of strolling toward the barn.'

Ben was caught in a tense silence. 'Then what?' he pressed.

'Nothing. That's all.'

'Didn't Halverson and Zuda come back to the house?'

'Oh, sure. Thought you was talking about

114

Lonnie. Park and Dave come wandering in after a little while. Must've stayed a spell in the yard where it was cooler. Pretty soon then everybody mounted up and rode off.'

'Lonnie had already left the place?'

'Been gone a half hour at least. Maybe more.'

'You know when he got back?'

Rufe stirred wearily. 'Don't see where none of this—'

'Do you?' Kyle insisted.

'Was asleep. Didn't see him or hear him, coming or going, for that matter. Trail leads off from back of the barn.'

Ben struggled to fit what he had learned together, could make no progress. Maybe he was at a dead end, but still . . .

'Mind if I take a look at my stew?' Rufe asked in a desperate voice. 'Don't want it scorching. Park's got a mighty fierce temper when things ain't just right, and if I try feeding him something burned no telling what he'd do . . . Why, once seen him knock a feller clean through that door there just for—'

'Go ahead, but mind how you do it.'

Kyle watched the older man add water to the kettle, stir slowly. 'Who found Lonnie?'

Rufe hesitated. 'Ain't sure, exactly. Some of the boys. They come running up here, yelling for the boss—'

'Early?'

'Little after sunrise. They'd gone to get their

horses so's they could saddle up, start hunting you again. Found him way in the back, behind some hay ... Been killed, then hid.'

The glimmer in Ben's mind blossomed suddenly into full light, and the stubborn pattern he had tried to assemble began to drop swiftly into place.

'The way he was killed—he was beat to death. That right?'

'Same as Bud. Hammered into nothing you've ever seen. Don't know if a club was used, or maybe a gun butt. Whatever, it sure was bad.'

Ben threw the cleaver aside. A river of fire was rushing through him, a need to bring the matter to a close, prove he was in the clear. He had the answer; he was sure of it.

'Where's Rocky Point from here?'

Rufe replaced the lid on the kettle, frowned. 'Due south ten mile or so ... What's it got to do—'

Ben caught the older man by the arm, pushed him back onto the chair. 'Stay there until you hear me ride off,' he snapped. 'Don't want any trouble with you.'

Wheeling, he kicked open the door and stepped into the yard. Reaching the sorrel, he went to the saddle and glanced back. Rufe was still seated. Spurring the red, he whirled away.

CHAPTER NINETEEN

Ben looked to the sun. Plenty of time to reach Rocky Point by the specified meeting hour. Best he used care, however, and not permit himself to get trapped again—keep to the brush, avoid open country unless there was no alternative.

He had to be right. Everything fit, and if there were a few gaps, he'd bluff. He'd be going it alone, he realized; not one man in the posse, sheriff and deputy included, could be considered a friend. He grinned tightly. What kind of fool was he, riding into the hands of a dozen or more enemies all searching for him with but one purpose in mind—a lynching?

I'd better be right! he thought grimly. But if not there wasn't anything left for him anyway.

He located Rocky Point a short time later. It was still a full mile or so distant and he halted on the fringe of a piñon-covered slope to give it thorough study. Would the riders be meeting below its ragged face, or on the plain at the summit?

He glanced again to the sun. Not far from noon. Some of the posse members could already be there. He settled his gaze on the upper flat, watched for several minutes. Seeing no movement either at that point or on the slope leading up to it, he concluded the gathering would most likely take place at the foot of the butte.

Accordingly, he swung the sorrel back into the grove of squat, scraggly trees, and rode a wide circle until he was to the front of the bluff. He encountered no one during his approach, but when he was finally in position to see clearly, he discovered a dozen or more men on hand.

Drawing in close, he made a quick count . . . fourteen riders. He thought such represented the entire posse but he could not be sure.

However, Halverson was there; and Zuda, Tom Dane and Sheriff Guyman. Some of the men were hunkered against the base of the cliff, hats pushed to the backs of their heads. Others squatted in the meager shade offered by clumps of rabbit-brush, sage and other gray-green shrubs. The horses were picketed a distance to their right.

He'd have to gamble on there being others yet to arrive, Ben decided, and continuing his wide circle until he had placed the horses between the men and himself, cut in and made his way to that point.

Dismounting, he checked his pistol for loads, and then, bent low, he worked his way quietly through the undergrowth and scattered rocks to where he crouched at the edge of the small level where the party had assembled.

'My guess is he's left the country, gone for good,' a small, thin man in a wrinkled business suit was saying. 'Can't tell me one of us wouldn't have seen him, was he still around.'

'Deputy saw him this morning,' Halverson snapped impatiently.

'My point,' the thin man replied. 'I figure he pulled out right when he learned we'd found Lonnie. What do you think, Tom?'

The deputy, hunched on his heels only a few paces from where Ben hid, scratched at the ground with a twig. He shook his head.

'Kyle ain't the running kind—and he claims he didn't kill Bud or anybody else.'

Park Halverson rose to his feet. 'You calling me a liar?' he demanded angrily.

Dane shrugged. 'Nope, just telling you about Kyle, and how he feels about it.'

Walt Guyman, next to Dane, waved the rancher back. 'Simmer down, Park. Tom's only trying to do a job, same as me.'

Kyle swept the group with a calculating glance. The men were fairly well bunched, but holding them with a single gun would be touchy. He wished now he'd kept one of the weapons he'd taken from Ollie and Clete, but it hadn't occurred to him then.

'Well,' a lanky puncher said, rising and stretching lazily. 'Say what we're going to do. My tail's getting mighty sore pounding that leather.'

Ben Kyle cocked the hammer of his forty-five, pulled himself upright. 'You can stop looking,' he said quietly. 'I'm here.'

There was a quick rustling sound as the startled men sprang to attention. All movement ceased instantly as Ben's flat voice again sliced through the dry heat.

'Enough of you there to cut me down—I know that. But my gun's on Halverson. He'll die same time I do.'

The big rancher was staring at him, lips working convulsively as anger racked his frame. Nearby, arms hanging loosely at his side, body slightly bent forward, stood Dave Zuda. Kyle eyed the man coolly.

'Better tell your killer and everybody else,' he said to Halverson, 'to keep their hands out where I can see them unless they want you dead.'

The rancher nodded abruptly. 'You heard him,' he snapped.

All but Zuda relented, settling back, crossing their arms over their chests or hooking their thumbs in their belts. The gunman did not stir, remained poised as if to strike. Walt Guyman wheeled slowly to Kyle.

'Must have something mighty important to say, wading into this whole bunch like you are.'

'I have,' Ben answered.

'Then you'll get your chance,' the old lawman said, and dropped back to where he was abreast Kyle. 'Go ahead.'

Halverson had recovered his poise. 'Sure, killer, go right ahead. But it'll be the last talking you'll ever do.'

'Maybe,' Kyle said softly. 'I'm telling you all again, I never murdered Bud, or Lonnie Rand either, no matter how it looks to you. Last I saw of Bud was in Carmody's that night. And Lonnie—I went to Halverson's to talk to him yesterday and run into you. Was the last time I saw him, too.'

'Takes proof to make us believe that,' the rancher said. 'You got some?'

'Not the kind you're looking for, but here's a couple of other things. Guess you're all pretty well set that the same man killed them both since they were beat up bad.'

'Worst I've ever seen,' a bearded puncher said, shaking his head. 'Nothing but blood everywhere.'

'Must've been the same man,' another agreed.

'Just how I figure it. Now, here's something you maybe don't know,' Kyle continued. 'Night before Lonnie was found dead in the barn, Halverson and Zuda went in there with him.'

'How do you know?' the rancher demanded, bristling.

'Rufe, your cook. Had a long talk with him. You deny it?'

Halverson's eyes flamed. 'That Goddamn flabberlip, I'll—' he began and then shrugged. 'Hell, no. Never said I—did. Lonnie was crabbing about being cooped up. I was keeping him safe, out of your way. He wanted to go to

121

town, get himself drunk.'

'You let him?'

'Sure, figured maybe there wasn't no harm in it because we had you holed up somewhere in the hills. Me and Dave just walked him to his horse, that's all. Was hot and we was getting some air.'

'And Lonnie got on his horse and went into Oak Springs.'

Halverson bobbed his head. 'Come back about midnight.'

'You're a liar,' Kyle stated evenly. 'I was in town all night. I saw everybody that rode in or rode out. Rand wasn't one of them.'

The rancher's face darkened. 'Just talk. Ain't nobody taking a killer's word. Truth probably is that you never was in town.'

'There's proof of that,' Tom Dane said, coming into the conversation. 'He holed up in that old building where the Caverlys had a shop. His horse was seen standing out behind the place early in the evening, was still there around three in the morning.'

'How you know that?' Guyman asked, arms settling against his sides.

'Pete Henderson come to the office in the morning, reported it. Said he figured some drifter was sleeping in the place and we ought to watch out, that a fire might get started.'

Interest began to show on the faces of several men. The thin man in the dusty suit removed his hat, scratched at his balding head.

'Then if Lonnie never did leave Halverson's—'

'He was killed when he went to get his horse,' Ben said. 'Only Zuda and Halverson were with him. I figure one or the other did it to keep him from talking to me ... And, considering the way he was killed—beat to death—my guess is that Halverson's the murderer.'

CHAPTER TWENTY

Only the dry clacking of insects in the dead heat interrupted the strained hush.

Park Halverson's face changed to a sickening purple. His fists began to clench, unclench. 'Why—why you Goddamn saddle tramp—'

'Halverson himself?' Walt Guyman said in a disbelieving voice. 'Lonnie—and his own son?'

Ben nodded. He was treading thin ice, trying to bridge the gaps. 'Maybe Bud was an accident. Wouldn't know. Lonnie because he could tell the truth. And I was handy and became the goat. Wanted me out of the way so's he could get my pa's land. Would've worked nice for him.'

'Damnedest mess I ever heard!' Halverson broke in. 'Now, why would I—'

'You've got a hell of a temper,' Kyle said calmly, 'and you think you're a big man with

123

your fists. When Bud didn't take me there on the Flat, and again later in Carmody's, you lost your head—'

'Dave!' Halverson yelled suddenly and, throwing himself to one side, grabbed for his pistol.

Ben drew and fired instantly, saw the rancher stagger. In that same fragment of time Walt Guyman's weapon blasted, its sound blending with the report from Zuda's pistol.

'Stay put everybody!' Dane shouted, and leaped into the center of the circle.

The man in the business suit glanced to the deputy, wheeled, knelt beside Halverson. After a moment he shook his head. He turned then to Zuda.

'Still alive,' he said. 'Not for long, I expect.'

Dane crossed to where the gunman lay. 'Dave, you ain't got much time. Was it the way Kyle said?'

Zuda stirred. 'Park dead?'

The deputy nodded. 'What about it?'

'Was the way Kyle said ... Tried to pull him off the boy but he was plumb crazy...'

'And Lonnie?'

'Was scared he'd talk, tell about it.'

A long sigh of relief slipped through Ben Kyle's lips. Holstering his weapon, he turned to Guyman.

'Sheriff, I'm obliged to you for siding with me. Zuda had me cold. If you—'

He checked his words, stared at the old

lawman. Guyman's face was chalk white and one hand was clamped to his side. Blood was oozing through his fingers.

'Deputy!' Kyle shouted. 'Over here! The sheriff's hit.'

The crowd wheeled, hurried to where Ben and the lawman stood. At that moment Guyman began to sink, his knees giving way slowly. Finally he was sitting. Dane and several others straightened the older man out, laid him back full-length.

'Get a horse over here!' the deputy yelled. 'Got to get him to the doc.'

Guyman's eyes fluttered; a hard grin pulled at his lips as he moved his head slightly.

'Too late for that, boy,' he murmured. Reaching up, he unpinned his badge, pressed it into Tom Dane's hand. 'You been after this ... Take care ... of it.'

The old lawman's body went lax. Dane rose slowly, eyes riveted to the star. After a moment he looked up, glanced about the ring of silent men.

Ben gauged the stricken depths in the man's eyes. The words, *What you wanted, isn't it?* sprang to his lips. But he let them die. Tom Dane would wrestle with his conscience in the days and nights to come without being prodded into it.

Nodding to the men, he turned away, started for the sorrel. He had a lot of work to do, getting the ranch in shape ... And then there

125

was Melinda Melrose to think about.

126

We hope you have enjoyed this Large Print book. Other Chivers Press or G. K. Hall Large Print books are available at your library or directly from the publishers. For more information about current and forthcoming titles, please call or write, without obligation, to:

Chivers Press Limited
Windsor Bridge Road
Bath BA2 3AX
England
Tel. (01225) 335336

OR

G. K. Hall
P.O. Box 159
Thorndike, Maine 04986
USA
Tel. (800) 223–6121 (U.S. & Canada)
In Maine call collect: (207) 948–2962

All our Large Print titles are designed for easy reading, and all our books are made to last.